D1168847

Mind Blowing
True Ghost
Stories

Signs From
The Afterlife

Carl Buehler

Copyright © 2010 Carl Buehler
All rights reserved.

ISBN: 1451579853
ISBN-13: 9781451579857

PROLOGUE

Since I was a young child, I have had a burning desire to discover what happens to a spirit after it has left the shell of its earthly body. Is there a heaven or a hell and is that where our spirit goes? It's not about wanting to believe that there is a paradise or fire and brimstone. It goes much deeper than that; it's about wanting the answers that no one really knows. Is there really another world, another place, or a parallel universe, and can our spirits actually live on forever? Throughout my life I have had to bear the pain of friends and loved ones and people I knew only briefly passing on. With each passing year, my quest and passion for answers has increased, and I am happy to say that, because of my experiences of the past few years, I am now positive that, when we die, it is not the end of the story. As time goes on and I am able to collect more evidence and continue to have amazing experiences, it solidifies my belief that there is another dimension, and it's all around us, all the time. All it takes to discover it is an open mind and the willingness to connect with it. My continuing journey has led me to believe that my loved ones are not gone forever and that perhaps, one day, they will be waiting to see me on the other side. In the meantime, if I am persistent enough, maybe I will have the good fortune to bridge the gap between life and death and make some connections; that is the nucleus of my story.

It all began in the spring of 2002.

I had been through two harsh divorces, my daughter had left for college in Florida, and my son was becoming more independent. It seemed like the perfect time to follow my dreams and, being close to forty, I knew that if I didn't go for it then, it would probably never happen.

Pulling out a map of the US, I searched for a destination where I thought I could live and be happy. It only took an hour for me to decide upon Lake Tahoe. That region had everything I desired. It had mountains, alpine lakes, forests, and desert, with the Pacific Ocean just a few hours away.

So, I packed my belongings, gathered my life savings, and headed across the Nation. The place I had lived my whole life, Dayton, Ohio, was behind me now. It's not a bad city, but I realized that I yearned for more than it could offer me.

As I approached my destination, I saw it was everything I had imagined and more.

Lake Tahoe is at an elevation of 6225 feet, with an average water depth of 1000 feet, surrounded by mountain peaks, which are snow capped at least half the year. The crystal-clear water reflects the color of the sky, which is blue and cloudless much of the time. The hues range from inky blue to turquoise, depending on the water depth, and sometimes, clouds reflect on the water, creating awe-inspiring sunsets of pinks, purples, and oranges. At times, the lake sparkles silver, reflecting a steely winter sky, the surrounding shores shrouded in a pristine white winter blanket. Then, on stormy days, when the mountains are concealed in clouds and the whitecaps are racing to the shore, it resembles the ocean and you can almost smell the salt. If there is a Heaven on Earth, Lake Tahoe is it!

Within a month, I had found a job at the Cal Neva Resort and Casino in Crystal Bay, Nevada. It was my first experience working in a casino, and the history of the place was just amazing. The views of Lake Tahoe and the surrounding mountains from the Cal Neva restaurant and hotel rooms are breathtaking. Frank Sinatra had owned the place in the early 1960s, and many celebrities, legends, and mobsters had visited over the years. Many biographies mention the Cal Neva, including those of Marilyn Monroe, The Rat Pack, Frank Sinatra, and Dean Martin. It has also been used as a location for several movies sets, including *The Godfather 2, Things Change,* and *Cobb.*

Chapter 1
CAL NEVA

At first, I thought the Cal Neva would just be a steppingstone into the job scene. However, I loved it so much, I ended up staying there for six years and counting. I began working at the world famous "Circle Bar" as a bartender . One day, I noticed a job posting on the bulletin board. The position was for a "Tunnel Tour Guide." It sounded interesting, so I put in my application and, before I knew it, I was hired for the job! At that time, I received a crash course on the history of the place and all its secrets. I was so fascinated that I decided to do some research on my own to verify everything I had learned. All the incredible happenings that had gone on had amazed me.

The Cal Neva was built in 1926 and has a fantastic history, both real and paranormal. Whether you are a believer or a non-believer, what I am about to tell you is the absolute truth! Many things I will tell you are unbelievable, but again, I say, it is all true.

It all started when I began my tunnel tours. First, I had to research and explore the property. That is when I began to learn the history of the underground tunnels. These tunnels were built when the Cal Neva was first constructed. They expand beneath and throughout the property and down to Lake Tahoe, it is said, for the purpose of bringing in illegal liquor during the prohibition days of the late 1920's.

Chapter 2
THE TUNNELS

My first incident took place down in the tunnels.

I remember vividly. It was a Saturday around 2 a.m. on June 5, 2004.

Toward the end of my shift, after a moderately busy Saturday night, there was no one at the bar and just a few customers left playing out on the casino floor. I decided to get ready to close up for the night and stock the bar with beer for the next day. I headed down the carpeted stairs behind the bar-lounge area and unlocked the door into one of the tunnels that runs under the property, where the beer cooler is located, below the bar. The memory is still vivid, it was dimly lit and eerily quiet in the tunnel that night, and there were no other employees around. The door leading to the beer room tunnel is always kept locked. I was the only one with the key that night.

I picked up a case of beer, locked the cooler door, and walked the few steps to the door that leads out from the passageway, back into the public area. Just before I could open it, a rattling sound caused me to turn and look back down the tunnel. It was the sound of a door handle turning and, out of the corner of my eye, I noticed something moving. Startled, my heart thumping, I stood transfixed, waiting to see if someone else was there. The sound came from a door about forty feet away on the right-hand side of the tunnel. It took about ten or fifteen seconds for the door to slowly open all the way. It remained open for about ten seconds, before it began to slowly close again and shut with a firm click. It was as if someone had opened it, walked through, and closed it, but there was not a soul in sight. I remained rooted to the floor in shock, with the hairs on the back of my neck bristling. After regaining my composure, I ran down the tunnel to the door, still carrying the case of beer, to investigate. I opened the door and looked in. It was pitch black inside, but when my eyes adjusted and with just enough light creeping in from the open doorway, I could see the small empty room with a concrete floor and no one inside. I quickly closed the door and hurried back out into the warmth and light of the casino to escape the cold chill that followed me.

There was no explanation for what had just occurred. It was very still in the tunnel; that door is inside the building, so it was not blown open by the wind, and there was no draft or vent of any kind nearby.

To this day, I still feel a chill every time I go down there, and I keep watching for that door to mysteriously open again.

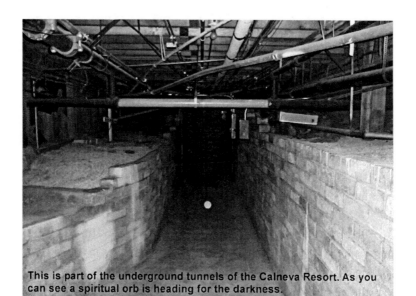

This is part of the underground tunnels of the Calneva Resort. As you can see a spiritual orb is heading for the darkness.

Chapter 3
THE CELEBRITIES

The Cal Neva Lodge is America's oldest originally-licensed casino. Most of the tunnels were the scenes of many illegal activities from the time it was built in 1926 to the early 1960s. The Cal Neva fire of 1937 burned the place to the ground, but luckily, the tunnels were spared the disaster.

When Frank Sinatra purchased the Cal Neva in 1960, he was told by the FBI and the Nevada Gaming Commission that if he were caught with certain mobsters in his casino at any time, he would be shut down and have his license revoked.

From 1960 to 1963, Frank Sinatra teamed up with a mobster, Sam Giancana (Who was said to be Sinatra's silent partner), to redesign and rebuild most of the tunnels. When rebuilt, the tunnels could reach cabins where major celebrities sometimes stayed. Those are now known as cabins 3, 4, and 5, which at times housed members of the "Rat Pack," Marilyn Monroe, and some of the Kennedy family. These tunnels also made it possible for the mobsters to move around at will, undetected.

Frank Sinatra also built the Frank Sinatra Celebrity Showroom, where he brought in the greatest performers, movie stars, and talent of the day. This is why it is believed that so much spiritual energy exists up on the showroom stage. More spiritual orbs are photographed on that stage than anywhere else on the property. Orbs are perfect circles, floating balls of light in various colors, that are said to be the spirits of the dead. They can appear on digital photographs but are, to my knowledge, also seen with the naked eye.

To the right of the stage is a balcony. There, any mobster or major celebrity who didn't wish to be seen could sit and watch the performances. They could see without being seen and enter and exit undetected through a tunnel, which led to either the cabins or the roof awaiting a helicopter. The Kennedy's were known to use this method, and "Ole Blue Eyes," if he needed to, could make a quick getaway. To this day, the helicopter pad is still there.

Orbs are everywhere inside the Frank Sinatra Celebrity Showroom. The stage has more paranormal activity than anywhere else on the property.

Chapter 4
THE SPIRITS

Many psychics have visited the Cal Neva, hoping to summons the spirits of the late Marilyn Monroe or Frank Sinatra.

During the winter of 2004, with a blanket of snow covering the area, a film crew from the British TV show, *Dead Famous*, arrived at the Cal Neva. They brought along a psychic, hopeful that they would get some indication that the spirits of Frank Sinatra and Marilyn Monroe were still around.

During the daylight hours, they went into Frank Sinatra's cabin but did not feel any extraordinary energy there. Once in Marilyn's cabin, the psychic said that he felt a strong presence and could feel it "whipping around the room."

They were also led into the tunnel that Frank Sinatra had redesigned, which allowed him to go secretly between the casino, his office, and his cabin, which connected through a door in the back of the closet.

The psychic then said he would like to go into the showroom at night to do some paranormal investigation. While looking around backstage, he said he felt a presence moving around and up the stairs, leading to the balcony above the stage. Soon after he went up the stairs, a feeling caused him to turn, and he instantly snapped a photo in that direction. The picture showed a streak of light trailing across it, appearing long and worm like; he said it might have been an orb traveling at extremely high speed.

Then the psychic decided, since he had not yet been able to feel Frank Sinatra's presence, it would be worthwhile to have a séance another night on the showroom stage. Late at night, in the darkness with the flickering light from a few candles casting eerie shadows, the showroom was an extremely creepy place.

There were several participants, including two members of the American Association of Electronic Voice Phenomena, a journalist, and some Cal Neva employees. They were all chanting Frank Sinatra's name when, all of a sudden, the psychic felt some kind of presence and asked "what is your name?" His body went tense and he fell back in the chair with his head forced back quite violently. Then he chanted in what was thought to be the native Washoe Indian dialect. Simultaneously, another participant screamed, "get out!" for no apparent reason. Then a new energy overcame the psychic, a softer, more relaxed character. He began rubbing his eye and acting as if he was smoking a cigarette; all his mannerisms then indicated Sammy Davis, Jr. (Sammy had lost his eye in a car crash and was always known to be holding a cigarette).

In fact, later, the psychic said Sammy Davis Jr. did channel through him and it was more than he had bargained for, since he had never channeled before. The group thought that the "get out!" had come from Frank Sinatra, since he was known for his quick temper. The psychic said that he thought Frank had sent Sammy to him, instead of being there himself!

I would not have been absolutely convinced, except for the fact that the psychic had spoken in the native tongue of the Washoe Indians. Not only did he have no idea who the Washoe Indians were, but he was speaking their language, without ever having learned it. I was amazed. After sending a copy of the videotape of the séance to some Washoe Indian chiefs living in the area, we had them translate it for us. The chiefs informed us that the Indian Spirit had spoken angrily and the message was for us to "get out!" (they do not want the casino here!). The land the Cal Neva was built on used to be a summer camp for the Washoe Indians, and it is said the parking lot was built over burial grounds.

Chapter 5
KEVIN'S GHOST

Another incident involved a good friend of mine, Kevin. He was the Cal Neva's Food and Beverage Manager.

It was around 3 a.m. on Thanksgiving night of 2005. Kevin was in his office, which is an old dressing room in the wings, right next to the Frank Sinatra Celebrity Showroom stage. The showroom can hold up to a maximum of 400 people, and the stage is about sixty feet wide. Kevin was catching up on paper work, all the doors were locked, and it was pitch black in the showroom with all the lights off. It is a creepy place indeed when no one else is around, especially in the gloom of the early morning hours.

Kevin said that while he was working, he got an uneasy feeling, as if someone or something was playing tricks on him and that he was being watched! All of a sudden, he heard the switch of his office light click off, and he was instantly shrouded in darkness. He jumped in fear and shock waves passed through his body as he realized there was no reason for anyone else to be around at that time. The only light now came from his cell phone and, looking around, he confirmed that he was indeed alone, ALL ALONE ! His fear felt like a sharp knife in the pit of his stomach, as he heard unusual sounds, perhaps footsteps, on the stage outside. Pulling himself together enough to get up from his desk, he ran out of his office and onto the middle of the stage. The instant he realized no one was there, he said he felt as if something walked right through him and he felt that he was NOT ALONE! He described it as nothing he had ever felt before, the coldest chill he had ever experienced. Not like a cold chill from freezing temperatures, but like the feeling of "something cold" passing right through his body. He was terrified and shaking and wanted to run but could barely move; his skin felt tight and cold. Then he realized his cell phone was still clutched in his hand and he aimed it, randomly taking pictures before retreating quickly back to his office. Sometime after he had switched the light back on and when his heart had finally stopped racing, he calmed himself down and settled back to the work at hand.

The cell phone pictures were put aside until the next day, when Kevin decided to take a look, the results sending shivers down his spine. He discovered an image of some kind of entity, grayish-white in color, with an outline of a body and even facial features. It looked as though it was holding some kind of weapon, like a spear, or the strap of perhaps a musical instrument over its shoulder. He could even see in detail where it was on the stage. I was awestruck! If there is such a thing as a ghost, it was pictured there!

Sadly, Kevin passed away on June 27, 2006, but a week before he died, I had the opportunity to talk to him. I told him that I would like to use his picture for my tunnel tours, but I needed to know that it was legitimate. Kevin looked me square in the eyes and told me that he had never believed in spirits or ghosts and had always thought the paranormal was a lot of hogwash. But he said his experience in the showroom and that picture had changed his life and his beliefs. A week later, Kevin fell asleep and never woke up under unknown circumstances. He was forty-five years old. Since that time, I have done research, talked to Kevin's family members, co-workers, and friends and, to this day, I really believe that this ghostly picture is authentic.

Chapter 6
FAMOUS CABINS

In recent years, séances have become a regular event at the Cal Neva. At first, we didn't know what we were getting into, but we have had some incredible things happen, so we continue to do them. That is what I want to talk about now.

A few months after Kevin's death, we decided to have our first employee séance. We did not expect much at first. We started out in the tunnels, then to the show-room stage, and then into Frank Sinatra's cabin # 5.

You might call this episode a coincidence, but this is only the tip of the iceberg. It was around 2 a.m., and we were in Frank's cabin holding hands and attempting to summon his spirit. We had been concentrating for at least ten minutes, when suddenly, one of the members of the séance screamed, "I FEEL A PRESENSE!" It was late and dark with all the lights out, and we all jumped out of our skins and felt very afraid at first. Then, one of the four of us in the room, Jamie, yelled, "FRANK, IF YOU ARE HERE, SHOW US A SIGN!" Within thirty seconds, there was an intense crash right outside the front door of the cabin. The noise was so loud, it sounded like a shotgun blast. It scared all of us very badly and Jamie screamed, announcing that she was out of there and wanted nothing more to do with this. The rest of us agreed and, as we ran outside, we noticed that a large tent pole had fallen down and caused that sound. It was as if it had been pushed over purposely to scare the living daylights out of us and, I have to say, if that was the case, it worked!

The pole was about ten yards from Frank's cabin; it was a calm and quiet night with no wind, and the moon was full and very bright. Frank's cabin is a little cottage, several yards from the main casino and hotel buildings, separated from them by the pool and a patio area. After investigation of the area outside, we realized it would have been impossible for someone to knock over the tent pole and leave the area, without being seen by us. The pole was in the center of where the cabins are located, and we were in view of the area within seconds of the sound and would have spotted any culprit before he or she would have had a chance to escape!

We even had a TV crew, News Channel 2 out of Reno, come to investigate the property on one occasion. When they visited Frank Sinatra's cabin, there was an anchorman, a cameraman and a psychic, as well as three Cal Neva employees present. At the moment, the psychic said she felt a presence of someone else in the room. The TV remote control suddenly lifted about four feet up off the dresser and then slammed down on to the floor. All six people present witnessed this and agreed that there was no explanation as to why it happened. The news crew documented this event.

We feel it is Frank's cabin 5 that has the most spiritual activity.

There are two cabins next to Frank's cabin. Cabin 4 was for Frank's guests, usually celebrities who would come to the Cal Neva Lodge to perform. Next to cabin 4 is Cabin 3, which is now the most famous cabin on the property. This is where Marilyn Monroe would stay. She actually had an overdose in that cabin the week before her death. On that occasion, she was saved, only to die a week later in Los Angeles. Of all the cabins on the property, Marilyn's is not only the most popular, but it's haunted too!! Several psychics have verified this to me.

There were four separate guests in 2006 that had to be moved from Cabin 3 into the main hotel tower, due to strange happenings. I spoke to all four, who said that lights switched on and off by themselves and that they saw ghostly figures in the room. They each had to be moved very late at night into the hotel. Now, once again, you might think this is coincidence, but these were four different guests on completely different occasions.

Frank's was cabin number 5. Most of the other celebrities stayed in cabin number 4. Most paranormal activity takes place in cabin 3 and 5.

This is our most famous cabin at the Calneva Resort. Cabin number 3# is where Marilyn Monroe stayed, she was here a week before she died. We get lots of paranormal activity in here.

Chapter 7
THE GHOST'S SPEAK

Now I'd like to talk to you about "EVPs." EVP stands for Electronic Voice Phenomenon. It works likes this; you take a cassette recorder and speak into it, at the same time recording your surroundings. The goal is to try and record voices other than your own or those of others present. In other words, it is an attempt to record voices from another frequency, while trying to speak to a spiritual entity and interact with it. These voices are not heard at the time, only when the recording is played back.

I will never forget when I got my first EVP recording. It was late Halloween night of 2007, just after midnight, the "witching hour." My friend and co-worker Jamie and I walked through the whole property taking recordings. Our last stop was Cabin 3, Marilyn's cabin. We were alone, just the two of us. I remember the events that occurred in detail. First, I tried to unlock the door with the key and couldn't. I tried several times but could not get the key to work. It was a moonlit night and the wind was calm. There were no people around at this time of night and no activity of any kind. I asked Jamie to wait there while I went to find another key. As I walked away, Jamie exclaimed, "No, you're not leaving me here all alone!"

I laughed and told her, "Ok, I'll wait. You go get the key!" This whole time my cassette recorder had been on, where I had set it down right in front of the cabin door.

While I waited, I took out my camera and took pictures. Then I walked around on the deck of the cabin asking Marilyn Monroe to speak to me. When Jamie got back with the key, we finally had success in entering the cabin. As we walked through the door, we mentioned to each other that we both felt some kind of presence inside. It was very dark and cramped inside, consisting of a small bedroom, closet, and a bathroom. We stayed in the cabin for about an hour taking pictures and recording on the cassette player.

The next day, I played back my recorder. Amazingly, at the time I was alone, while Jamie was getting a second key, a second voice came on the recording. You could hear me ask, "Marilyn, if you are here, speak to me." At that precise moment, a woman's voice, in plain English, said, "What are you doing? Why are you here?" I was astounded! At the time of the recording I heard nothing; it wasn't until I played the recording that I heard the voice of the entity. In the background was Jamie's voice, just after the entity spoke, yelling that she had a new key, suggesting that the other female voice on the recording was not hers.

Now, you may be skeptical about all this, but let me just say that I have all the proof I need to show you and make you a believer. These are all my personal experiences that I have made great attempts to prove or disprove myself. I am the first person to try to debunk each inexplicable event that I see, hear, or feel, and I am not trying to convince anyone, one way or another. All I know is that I didn't believe in the supernatural, until I began this and did some research. I just want to share my experiences with you. I have more EVPs I'd like to tell you about; this is only the beginning! But, for now, I want to change the subject for a while and let you know about Marilyn Monroe's haunted light.

Chapter 8
MARILYN'S HAUNTED LIGHT

There is one particular light, down in one of the tunnels beneath the Cal Neva, which is the only one in the whole place that switches itself on and off. There is no reasonable explanation for this. The light is supposed to stay on twenty-four hours a day, and there is actually no switch to operate it. It has been checked by several different electricians, who have all said that they checked or fixed it and that it should not go off again. Then the very next day, the light turns itself off again. It is a very strange phenomenon. We call this Marilyn's light and for very good reason. Adjacent to this light is an old staircase going up. The stairs leads nowhere, now, but at one time, a door at the top led into the casino area. The stairs have since been blocked off at the top, and the door, now in the hotel lobby, leads to a closet used as a ski locker. A few years ago, a well-known psychic was invited to visit and take a walk through the property with the intention of finding paranormal activity. While down in the tunnels, she stated that she saw Marilyn sitting on these steps crying, upset because she did not like the way she had been portrayed. That spot is only about ten feet away from the light!

At first, I thought this psychic was "off her rocker." However, five pictures were taken by various people at the time and one showed a beautiful ball of light, just where we had been told Marilyn was sitting. The psychic explained to me that this was Marilyn's spiritual orb. Since then, we have got many orbs in the same area that are bright and beautiful. They are perfectly round spheres of light, between golf ball and basketball size. They are usually white, but do come in different colors. I have seen one that looked like a red and green sun. They are not dust specs on the camera lens, which show up as blotchy and brown; they are luminous and bright.

This is Marilyn Monroe's haunted light.

Chapter 9
THE SEANCES

The more spiritual séances that I have been involved in, the more inexplicable events have occurred.

My partner Jamie and I decided to organize an employee séance on March 26th 2008. It turned out to be the most incredible spiritual séance we have ever participated in. There were six people on that occasion. Out of this group, one person in particular, Dustin, displays a special sensitivity and says he can actually feel, and sometimes see, the entities. He has an ability to channel these beings to talk through him. Again, at first , I was very skeptical, but all that changed on this night, when I really came to believe that, indeed, Dustin has a gift.

It was just about midnight. We put up a table on the Frank Sinatra Celebrity Showroom stage and lit three candles. Then we locked the doors and turned out all the lights. The showroom is a fair sized room and can hold up to 400 people. The five other attendees held hands, with the only light now coming from the candles. I set my cassette recorder in the middle of the table and proceeded to walk around the stage taking pictures with my digital camera. My hope was to capture pictures of orbs and whatever else I could, while the séance was in progress. The only way to see if any spiritual orbs have been stirred up is to photograph them.

As the séance progressed, I could sense a lot of energy coming from the table. It was extremely quiet when, all of a sudden, Dustin appeared to go into a trance and began speaking in an unknown voice. He said a name that was indiscernible and began speaking out of character, saying various things, including that he was from another place and time. He said that he had been in charge, until he was shot and killed. His voice became very angry, and he demanded to know why we were there. Then he spoke more softly and said that Jamie was very pretty, then began laughing in a deep tone completely outside his normal vocal range. This went on for several minutes, and it seemed to be taking away all his breath and energy, to the point that he sounded as if he were having an asthma attack. Finally, when the entity left Dustin, with a loud outburst he screamed, "I see a man by the doorway!" Jamie asked him what the man looked like and he screamed, in a terrified voice, "He is wearing black clothes and a white shirt and looks about six feet tall!" A few moments later, Dustin went running out of the room and was nowhere to be found for a couple of hours.

At that point, we decided to soothe our rattled nerves and get out of the showroom for awhile. We decided to go into the hotel next, into Room 101. I had heard that a suicide had taken place in that room, so we thought that it might be a good location to try next on our quest for spirits. The five of us that were left went in there for several minutes while I took pictures.

After that, we decided to go to Cabin 3 (Marilyn's). It was getting late, so we just stayed a few minutes there and then headed for home.

For some reason, I felt as though it was a night we would never forget! I was not disappointed. The next day, I went through my pictures and listened to the cassette recordings of the events of the night before.

What was caught on tape and in some of the photographs sends chills up my spine every time I see and hear them. Initially, when I was alone before the séance began, when I first started recording, there was a woman's voice on the tape. She spoke with a screech that scared the living daylights out of me! Our own voices on the tape were very distinguishable, so whose voice was this? About half way through the tape, while we were in Room 101, I am heard asking several questions. In one I ask, "Are you here spirit? Did you die here?" After a few seconds, in plain English, a soft voice said "Yesss...." Then, a little later on, as the tape progresses, we can all be heard talking again and Mark says, "I feel them, they want to be released." Then Jamie cries, "I feel them close, I am getting chills all over my body!" Then an entity shouts above all of us, in an angry, screaming voice, "GET OUT! GET OUT! GET OUT!" repeating for a full ten seconds. Then, after a slight pause comes another voice that is unaccounted for and it screams for another ten seconds, but those words we were unable to decipher.

Remember, at the time of the recording, we heard nothing out of the ordinary; it was only when the tape got played back that I could hear the voice of the entity. It obviously did not want us there!

After going through all of the photographs of that night them, I found that I had a lot of orbs on film. That did not surprise me so much. What shocked me to the core, however, was a picture taken in Room 101. After studying all the pictures carefully, I noticed in one the reflection of a man in the hotel room window. I recounted everyone who had been in the room with me and this image was absolutely not any one of them! The man was dressed in black pants and vest, with a white shirt; in fact, it was the very description of the man that had so terrified Dustin in the showroom. No one in our group had been wearing black and white. That image was not supposed to be there (or was it?). Also, everyone in our group had been positioned in a line facing toward the camera, and this image was in profile. Believe me, I went over and over it in my mind for a rational explanation, finally realizing that no one there could possibly have caused that reflection. To this day, it is still unexplained.

This picture was taken on the showroom stage in 2008. This ghostly figure (top right) showed up. It never appeared again.

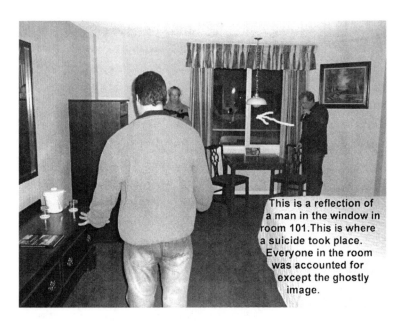

This is a reflection of a man in the window in room 101.This is where a suicide took place. Everyone in the room was accounted for except the ghostly image.

Chapter 10
THE GANGSTER

There was another incident that took place on stage in the showroom. I was alone. It was around 11 p.m. on September 2, 2008. I was speaking on my cassette recorder, attempting to get an "EVP." It was extremely dark up on stage. I had locked the doors and it was very creepy and quiet, with no one else around. I began taking pictures with my digital camera to see if I could get a few orbs. Ever since I started trying to get evidence of the paranormal, I seem to get stronger feelings when something is developing around me. I did not want to spook myself with negative thoughts and tried to remain calm. All at once, I felt a strong presence behind me. I spun around and started taking pictures; the feeling got stronger and stronger over the span of a few minutes; then, suddenly, it ceased. In all, I took about a hundred pictures but especially in the direction from which those feelings came.

Then I headed out of the showroom and into the casino, back to the bright lights and the comfort of the few employees that were still around at that time of night. I checked all the pictures and, sure enough, out of all of them, there was one that showed a man. He was standing a few feet away from me, dressed in black, appearing almost transparent; however, his features showed up in detail.

After my experience in the showroom that night and seeing that picture for the first time, I have to say that it really had an effect of me. I realized that something had actually been there behind me at the precise moment I felt it. I had been alone in a locked room. It sends shivers down my spine thinking about it now and my skepticism is definitely waning!

Chapter 11
THE WHITE DOORS

May 14, 2008 was a very special night, it was the tenth anniversary of Frank Sinatra's death.

At around one in the morning, up on the showroom stage with all the lights out and the doors locked, I had joined several other employees; our plan was to have a séance to communicate with Frank Sinatra on that particular night.

Several hours before the séance began, some of the lights in the showroom had been mysteriously switching on and off by themselves, with no possible explanation. We all felt a lot of energy in the showroom that night. By this time, we had performed several séances and felt that we were gaining experience and becoming increasingly adept at reaching the paranormal energy in the room. We had a table set up on the stage where three lit candles stood, which were our only source of light.

I realized quickly that spirits were attempting to come through, because I had several fully charged batteries in my camera go instantly dead. When this happens, it is a good sign that entities are draining the energy.

Before beginning the séance, we did a walk around to make sure that there would be no interference from any outside noises or obstacles and that we were the only people in the room. We checked for animals too, since we have had a raccoon problem in the past, making their homes in the roof and other nooks and crannies, and helping themselves to food from the kitchen! However, on this night, we found nothing we thought could hamper our efforts; then we shut and locked all the doors. The last door we shut was a double door at the back right of the stage, about thirty to forty feet from our table. These doors are behind the stage, leading to a storage area and are painted white, so even with it very dark, they are still visible.

There were four of us participating in the séance. We were all holding hands for about thirty minutes, then the tape on my recorder ran out, so I stopped to change it. The tape had been running for the whole time. Once I changed the tape, it got quiet, extremely quiet. We were chanting for Frank to show us a sign and were concentrating hard and speaking very softly. It was so bizarre; I vividly remember two people in the group trembling with fear and Jamie saying that she could feel something close by. One of the candles went out, so we only had two lit at that time, and it was very dark. As we were holding hands, we could feel the trembling of the others and, at this point, I knew something was going to happen, but what? There was intense electricity in the air, and I could see the fear in everyone's faces and feel the perspiration on the hands I held. We all waited in anticipation for whatever was about to take place. The recorder was still running, picking up everything, including our chanting and things that cannot be heard by the human ear.

My concern was that anyone at anytime was going to jump up and run out of the room in pure fear. Fortunately, we all kept our composure, but just when I thought things were starting to calm down, there was one last gasping scream, "Frank show us a sign!" At that moment, the two white doors burst open with an intense crash, as if someone had bolted through them in a frenzy. We all jumped up in complete shock and gut wrenching fear; two of us instinctively ran toward the doors looking for some sort of reasonable explanation. Instantly, we realized that the doors had no possible way of opening, unless they were pushed with some force. They are inside doors leading to a room about thirty feet long, with no other doors or windows inside, so there was no wind or draft and no way someone could run through without becoming trapped inside. The only way out is to come back the way you came in.

To this day, there are four people who cannot explain what happened that night. The next day, I listened to my cassette recorder and sure enough, I could hear very easily the doors slamming open. I have held on to that evidence to this day and have still not come up with any kind of earthly explanation for the phenomenon that occurred that night. Perhaps Frank really did not want to be bothered!

These are the doors that slammed open by themselves on May 14th, 2008 the 10th year anniversary of Frank Sinatra's death.

Chapter 12
GOLDHILL

Several friends and I decided to take a trip to Virginia City, which is known for much history and paranormal activity. When it was first discussed, about ten people said they were interested in going, but we ended up with a group of just four. We set the date for a Sunday in early November 2008 and made reservations to stay the night at the Gold Hill Hotel, about two miles outside of Virginia City. The hotel was constructed sometime before January 1862, although the exact date is uncertain. It was an important part of the thriving metropolis of Gold Hill and the nearby business and industrial center then known as Virginia. The population of the two towns combined was almost 40,000, making it one of the largest cities in the West at that time. Major mining operations in the area were producing large amounts of silver and gold, creating a boom that continued through the 1870s, but by the 1930s, the population had dwindled to only a few hundred people.

From Lake Tahoe to Virginia City it is about a one-hour drive. I traveled with Jamie and one other female friend. We met the other, a male friend in his mid forties, around 9 p.m. at the Gold Hill Hotel. A shining moon lit the sky that night, and it was calm with very little wind. Upon arrival, we did some research on the hotel and local area, by talking with the owner and some of the staff members. We learned that the room I was sharing with my male friend was haunted by the female spirit of a woman who had died in there. The story goes that she was a prostitute who was murdered by a local miner.

There is a mineshaft on the property, just a few yards from the hotel, which was the location of terrible tragedy in the late 1800s. Thirty-seven miners died in a cave inside that shaft, as well as the fire chief who went underground in an attempt to rescue them. We were told that the fire chief had slept in the room, which Jamie and our other friend occupied on the night of our visit, and we were excited to realize that both rooms we were to sleep in that night had such a color-ful history. We all hoped that we were in a great loca-tion to begin our quest for paranormal activity, which we began by taking a few photographs in our rooms. In no time, we were happy to discover that we had cap-tured several orbs.

We were also told that two young children had been playing outside, on a cold winter night sometime in the early 1900s, got lost, and unfortunately, froze to death. The hotel staff told us that many guests have reported the sound of children laughing and playing outside their hotel room doors late at night but, of course, upon investigation no one was there.

All of this information we were told is very interest-ing, but what I experienced for myself will blow your mind! Just to reiterate, I will not write down any of my experiences that I do not believe to be real, and I have debunked many pictures and weird happenings already that I have come across in my own research. What I am about to tell you is the story of an incredible journey into the paranormal world!

At around 10 p.m., we were all set to go ghost hunting, with two cassette recorders, a video camera, and three digital cameras in hand. We mentioned to the lady behind the bar at the hotel that we were heading to the Virginia City cemetery, known as Silver Terrace Cemetery. On hearing this, she suggested that we first visit their local cemetery in Gold Hill, at American Flats, about half a mile down the road. So, we jumped into one of our four-wheel drive trucks and headed off on our adventure. We found the dirt road we had been directed to quite easily, but we could not find the cemetery at first. We drove on for a few minutes and eventually decided to turn around. When we did, we noticed an iron fence; we had found the cemetery. Driving around to the gate we found it was wide open, which we found rather disconcerting, as if it was waiting for us. It was around 11 p.m., as we entered, and clouds partially concealed the silvery moon.

The graveyard is about a quarter of a mile long and a hundred yards wide. Now, being in the town of Gold Hill had been spooky enough, but this was something else; it was like going back in time to the 1800s into the old west, very open and spread out. The cemetery was way out in "no man's land" with nothing else there but a few far-away lights from distant homes. It reminded me of an old Hollywood horror movie scene in an ancient graveyard, late at night, the viewers gripping their chairs, anticipating the zombie that is about to come rising up out of a grave or the monster about to leap from behind a tree or the giant vampire bat about to come flapping by.

My imagination was running amok, and I could feel chills running up and down my spine. I knew we were all feeling quite scared about being there, but we were on a mission and no matter how afraid we felt, we needed to be where the spirits were, if we wanted to get any results. I can honestly say I was terrified, but I did not want to convey it to the others and get them more spooked. I knew that my male friend was a rookie and did not know what to expect. Of the women, one seemed to have more sensitivity to the paranormal, and Jamie gets quite fearful, but despite that, she comes along anyway on many of my expeditions.

I started my cassette recorder, and then began to take pictures; not surprisingly, there were orbs all over the place. I considered myself the veteran of the group, as I feel I have had the most experience in bringing out spirits, so I separated from the others and went off alone for a while, walking about fifty yards away. My main purpose was to make sure that, if I got any interesting pictures or EVPs, I would have more factual proof of the supernatural if I were alone, without other people in range, whose voices or images might confuse things.

There were hundreds of tombstones of various shapes and sizes, some surrounded by small fences, others lying flat on the ground, forgotten. Most of the graves were from the 1800s, and many contained young children, causing me to feel deep sadness.

It was cold and dark by that time, the only light coming from my camera flash. I had my camera in one hand and my cassette recorder in the other, all the while talking to the spirits. It is necessary when trying to obtain EVPs to talk to the spirits, just as if you are talking to another person, asking questions, etc. For example, when I came upon the grave of a Civil War veteran, I asked whether he had fought for the North or the South and what the name of his General was. While taking pictures around the graves of small children, I asked them if they would like to play a game, or if they needed me to help them in anyway. This is very significant, because of what occurred later on during the night.

It could have been my imagination, but while I was walking alone amongst those tombstones and reading the words that were inscribed on them, I felt a deep connection with each person buried there. After asking them if they missed their families, I felt sorrow that was hard to contain, as I wondered what they were like, how they had lived, and whether they had the same kind of thoughts, feelings, and dreams I have. Many families had been buried together, and some of the children were very young; siblings had died only a few years apart; brothers and sisters were buried side by side. My heart broke, realizing they had never experienced growing up, falling in love, getting married, having children of their own, and growing old. And is there anyone alive that still cares that they are there? It appears that I do; they have touched me deeply; my earlier fear had been replaced by extreme sadness. Then I came back into the present and decided it was time to reconnect with my group of friends. When I caught up to them, my cassette recorder was about to run out, which told me we had spent an hour in that cemetery. The others were getting cold and, now, back in the present, I realized I was too. So we decided it was time to move on to our next location, the expansive cemetery of Virginia City.

This is part of the mining shaft where 37 miners died along with a fire chief. This is in the small town of Goldhill.

Chapter 13
SILVER TERRACE CEMETERY

The first burial in Virginia City cemetery took place in the early 1800s. After the Comstock Lode was discovered and the booming mining camp developed into a more permanent settlement, it was decided that a cemetery was required. The cemetery actually consists of eleven original cemeteries that were memorials to the rich and also the culturally diverse groups that labored in the mines. When Virginia City was at its height of prosperity, the cemeteries were Victorian parks, well maintained and full of shrubs and flowers, a lovely oasis amid the arid desert landscape. Now, only rocks, sagebrush, and gnarled trees remain.

When visitors get into town, which is on the top of a hill, they can look down and see the whole cemetery. Driving through town is again like going back in time. It has old saloons, hotels, an opera house, wooden sidewalks, and many other structures dating back to the 1800s. Vehicles driving through town and the paved roads are the only things that indicate the reality of the present day.

It was around midnight when we drove toward the cemetery. Anticipating that the gates would be locked, we parked some distance away and began walking on a dirt road that led around the perimeter of the cemetery. This road was extremely wet and muddy, and I felt sorry about dragging everyone else along, so we decided that they would go back to the car and drive to the cemetery gate and I would meet them inside. I set off along the muddy, dark trail, alone; it was about

200 yards further up and downhill to my destination, the cemetery fence.

What had I been thinking? Here I was alone, after midnight, about a mile from the safety of my friends in a cemetery in the middle of nowhere! I felt a little insane for what I had undertaken, but I knew this was what I had come to do, no matter how afraid I felt. Finally, I arrived at the iron fence that encircled the cemetery, and I squeezed through a gap where two of the iron pickets were loose, crawling on my hands and knees, getting wet and dirty. At last, I was inside!

As I approached the first headstones, I could see that they were of all different types: decaying wood or metal, some carved out of stone and crumbling. Many of the burial plots in the cemetery are fenced or bordered, which was common practice during the Victorian era. Approaching the highest point of the cemetery, on top of the hill, there is a large statue of a man who died over a century ago, a sentinel of the entire place, I thought, silently watching over them all. It was at this moment that the reality of my solitude hit me, and I began to feel increasingly terrified of where I was. I barely felt the cold; by that time, the temperature had dropped to around 30 degrees Fahrenheit, the air was crystal clear and calm; there was no wind or clouds, with the moon supplying just enough light for me to pick a path among the headstones. As I stood in the middle of this huge place, an inner voice boomed, "I AM ALL ALONE!" and I found I was trembling, not from the cold, but out of pure fear. From the top of the hill, I could see the entire town in the distance with just a few twinkling lights. My cassette recorder was running the whole time, and I had been recording a play-by-play of my progress and snapping pictures simultaneously. Later on, while playing back the tape and discovering whatever else had been picked up, I relived the terror once again upon hearing it in my voice.

About a quarter of a mile away, I could just about make out the entrance to the cemetery, where the rest of the group was supposed to have entered. However, I saw no sign of any vehicle parked there. Despite feeling afraid, I refocused on the task at hand. I had a mission to accomplish, which was to communicate with the spirits, and I began pressing them to show themselves in some way. I am aware that the mind can play tricks on a person, especially when he or she is afraid, but I remained calm and honed in on my surroundings, my ears sharpened with every sound. By this time, my eyes had adjusted to the dark, and I could easily make out the tombstones illuminated by the moon. About thirty minutes had passed and then one of the most terrifying moments of my life began. It seemed to me that the whole cemetery was starting to come alive: I heard soft whispers and moans and saw shadows moving out of the corners of my eyes. Then I heard the sound of gravel crunching, which seemed to be about fifty yards away, like footsteps coming towards me. The sound made me jump, and I thought perhaps it was someone from my group approaching, so I waited. The footsteps went on for about forty-five seconds and sounded heavy enough to be a person, not an animal. As I stood there, the steps got closer and closer. I even thought that it might be a policeman sneaking up on me, since I was there illegally after closing time. Then everything went silent again, and I saw that no one was there. Later on, when I played the tape back, I heard myself say several times that I could hear footsteps, with the sound of gravel crunching in the background.

Once I had calmed down, after the footstep incident, I decided to talk to some of the tombstones, in an attempt to get some voices other than mine on the recorder (EVPs). I did that for a while, but I wouldn't know the results, until I played back the tapes later. Eventually, I decided I had better start heading to the entrance to look for my friends. While I was walking the quarter mile to the gate, I began to get the strongest feelings that, again, the cemetery was coming to life. I took several more pictures and then got a strong urge to run right out of the place, but my feet felt like lead, and I could not do it. I kept walking at the fastest pace I was allowed, telling myself how crazy I was to have come in alone. So many jumbled emotions ran through my head, as if all the spirits were trying to communicate with me at the same time.

Finally, I was at the entrance and my friends were there in the car. I screamed at them, "WHERE THE HECK WERE YOU GUYS?" They said they had been too cold and scared to leave the car and I said, "How do you think I felt?"

By this time, it was 2 a.m., and we decided to see if there were any saloons or anything else open in town. We found a 24-hour casino in the middle of town and stopped in to have a drink, all four of us glad to be back in the warmth and bright lights. I remembered that the well renowned Washoe Club was just up the street; it is supposed to be one of the most haunted places in Nevada. Several ghost hunters and psychics have reported the place to be very active, and I had recently seen a program about it on television. So, I decided to take a walk up the street to investigate and take a few pictures in front of the building, leaving the others behind at the bar. As I walked along the wooden sidewalks, I realized that I was, once again, all alone; no one else was out at that time of night. It seemed just like a ghost town. Camera in hand, I took several pictures of the town's old saloons, churches, and other structures. When I reviewed the pictures later, I saw some unbelievable things. In front of the Washoe Club, I took a few more pictures, and I could tell that the building was completely deserted or derelict. When featured on the "Ghost Hunter" show, it showed that the upstairs had been blocked off from the rest of the building and all the rooms were bare. There were no lights on, and it was so dark that while I was taking pictures, I could hardly make out the building on the camera screen.

After several minutes, I decided to head back and rejoin the gang, and we all agreed that we were tired and ready to return to our hotel. Once again parked in front of the Gold Hill Hotel, looking over at the old mine shaft, it struck me how incredibly tragic it must have been to lose the thirty-seven miners right there in that exact spot. Again, a wave of extreme emotion came over me. Despite the fact that we were tired and ready for sleep, we decided to set up cassette recorders and take more pictures in our rooms, just in case we were fortunate enough to capture anything of the paranormal during the night. What I did in fact find the next day amazed me!

This is the Virginia City Cemetery. On November 11th, 2008 at 1am while I was investigating this site, the graveyard came to life.

Carl Buehler

This is Virginia City , Nevada with part of the cemetery.

Chapter 14
DISCOVERIES FROM THE GRAVE

What I am about to tell you is all backed up with evidence I have collected in pictures and cassette recordings. Remember, while we were in the American Flats cemetery, just a half mile from our Goldhill Hotel, I was alone most of the time, having separated myself from the rest of the group.

The following morning, when quickly looking through the many pictures I had taken during the night (in my camera), I noticed that all the backgrounds were black. Upon returning home later that day, I downloaded the pictures to my computer to enlarge them and adjust the brightness and contrast to bring out more detail.

In one picture, which I had taken in an area where several children had been buried in American Flats Cemetery, there was a large tombstone in the foreground. Amazingly, in the background, previously unseen until the picture was enlarged and lightened, was the figure of a small child looking at me questioningly, as if to say "what are you doing here?" She (I thought it looked to be a female between five or six years old) was dressed in clothing that appeared to be of the 1800s era—a dress draped to the ground with a collar, the folds and creases in the fabric obvious, and shoes that appeared to be of the same vintage; I was struck at the details. The girl was very tiny in height, with hair, nose, and eyes all in proportion. I have a plan to one day go back to the exact location, to find her grave, so that I can put a name to this little girl's image.

The next incredible piece of evidence I want to talk about came from the Virginia City cemetery. Out of over a hundred pictures I took during that hour I was there alone, two photos showed a phenomenon known as ectoplasm. This is when an entity is trying to form itself into some sort of shape, whether human or otherwise, or it could be the residue left by a spirit recently in the area. Now, keep in mind that on that night there were no fires to create smoke, no fog or smog of any kind, nothing that I could see or smell at the time. It was a crisp, cold, and clear night, with low humidity, no wind, and a well-lit moon, and when I took those pictures, I didn't notice anything out of the ordinary. On reviewing the pictures on my computer, I wondered if I'd been there earlier or stayed longer, I might have discovered the image of a full blown apparition. There is no other explanation for the phenomenon on the photo that I can think of.

The entire time I was in the cemetery, I had my cassette recorder running. While listening to the recording the next day, I did find some interesting EVPs. One occurred at the time I was speaking to the tombstone of a man named "John" in the same vicinity where I had heard the footsteps. I had asked John if he was here with me and was he willing to talk? At this point in the recording, I heard several moans that I cannot explain. Then, when I asked some Civil War veterans "who is your President?" the response "Abe" was caught on my recording. Thankfully, at the time, I had heard nothing, except those footsteps, as it would have probably pushed me completely over the edge and out of that cemetery!

After I had decided to take a walk outside of the Virginia City saloon, in the middle of town around 2 a.m., while leaving my friends at the bar, I found I had discovered more evidence of the paranormal. As I was walking along the wooden sidewalks that night, I had noticed that there was no one else around, it truly felt like a ghost town at that hour, It was just me clutching my cassette recorder in one hand and camera in the other.

The following day, while reviewing the pictures I had taken of the old 19th century structures of Virginia City's main street, I was surprised and pleased to find that an unexpected image had appeared in one them. There was an old man standing across the street from me; he had a long grey beard and hair to match. He was dressed just like the old miners we had seen displayed in pictures on the walls of some of the old saloons and casinos in town. What really shocked me about it was the fact that it was very cold at the time, around 25 degrees, I would guess. I remember shivering in my warm jacket, but the man was not wearing a coat, just standing there in his shirt sleeves watching me. I truly believe that he was not of this earth! I don't think any warm-blooded human being could have endured the cold in those clothes. Most people would have been hurrying to find warmth, not just standing there like a statue.

On reviewing the photographs I had taken of the old Washoe Club, about a hundred yards farther up the street from where the "old miner" stood, there was another surprise. After enhancing the brightness of the pictures on my computer, I was amazed to see that, in one of them, there was a man looking out a window on the top floor. I knew the building was supposed to be deserted. As the owner had mentioned on the *Ghost*

Hunter program, he was the only person with a key, and there was only one way in, and that door was always kept locked. In addition, I asked several people around Virginia City if the Washoe Club had any occupants upstairs, and they had all confirmed that it is completely locked up and that no one lives there.

I remembered that, while taking the pictures, I had trouble focusing on the building as it was so black, and it was easy to tell that it was cold and uninhabited. The man in the window, the top third from the right to be exact, had a thick, handlebar moustache in the fashion of the 1800s that shows up again and again in the old pictures adorning the walls around town. He was there, staring down at me and, in a split second, was gone again, I know this because I had taken five similar pictures concurrently, and his image only appeared in one.

The little girl in the cemetery. This picture was taken on November 11th 2008 just outside of Virginia City.

Here is more ectoplasm taking shape into a ghostly form. The night was clear with no fog or smoke. It was taken on November 11th, 2008.

This is a picture of what I believe to be ectoplasm. It's when a ghost starts transforming into a shape such as a human or some type of form.

This is the picture of the old miner. I believe he was one of the miner's who died inside the mineshaft killing 37 miners just outside of Virginia City.

You can see a man looking out of the top 3rd window from the right. If you look close enough you can see he has a bicycle handlebar's mustache from the late 1800s. I took a second pic. and he was gone.

Chapter 15
MORE SÉANCES

On November 21, 2008, I arranged another séance in the Frank Sinatra Celebrity Showroom at the Cal Neva Resort. This time, there were seven people involved and, for the first time, we decided to open up the trap door on stage and explore the tunnel below. This tunnel had been used in the past for access to the cabins hundreds of feet away, but now only goes about a hundred feet, due to its collapse; the walls that have since been built to block it off. Once down there in the dark, we found stacks of newspapers dating as far back as the 1960s and the days of Sinatra's ownership. Despite the fact that we didn't feel any major paranormal activity that night, we discovered an amazing EVP while playing back my cassette recorder afterwards. About half way through the tape, we heard an entity trying to build up enough energy to come through, causing major static on the recording. During the first ten seconds it blurted out loud gasps; this was the point at which I realized it was not any of us, and then, in plain English, we heard the spirit shout, "She's a bitch!" It was chilling and inexplicable! A few minutes earlier on the tape, we had heard what could have been the same entity attempting to come through, but it takes a lot of energy for that to happen. Sometimes, it is hard to decipher the words, and only static is audible, so I will not assume that to be a fact.

We decided to have another séance at the Cal Neva on December 11, 2008, only this time we invited some professionals from the Nevada Paranormal Institute, who have been investigating the paranormal for many years. They brought with them some state-of-the-art equipment, including infrared cameras and electro-magnetic field (EMF) readers. The EMF readers pick up any variations in room temperature, hot and cold spots, and energy in the surrounding areas, possibly caused by an entity.

There were nine people in attendance, including one psychic and some members from the NPI. Several cameras were set up on the stage of the Frank Sinatra Celebrity Showroom, and we had cassette recorders running. On this occasion, we had more equipment set up than at any other time, to cover all angles, with highly sensitive cameras able to detect much more. Two men ran the equipment, while seven of us partici-pated in the séance, which began at about 10 p.m. As usual, all the doors had been locked and all the lights were out, and even with all those people there I could feel the fear and anticipation in the air.

We sat around a large, heavy circular table in the middle of the stage, with the seven of us holding hands. After a while, I mentioned to the friend next to me that I could tell she was feeling something com-ing through. The others at the table asked me how I knew, and I told them in a humorous way that she was " breaking my hand!" For a split second, the tension was broken; everyone laughed, and my friend relaxed her grip. As the night progressed, we all asked ques-tions of the spirits, hoping we would get some kind of response, at least on the cameras or recorders. When I asked the spirits to show me some kind of sign, at the same instant I got a jab, just like something stick-ing me, right in my neck. I immediately yelled for the spirit to do that again, or even worse, to kick or punch me. I'm a very skeptical person, so I knew that if it really was a spirit, then it could do it again. If it didn't physically touch me, then I had to rule it out as just my imagination. After a few minutes went by, I knew that it must have been just that and I felt a little disappointed, but anyway the night was still young.

An hour into the séance, I felt that this might not be the night we had hoped for, but boy was I wrong. We were, in fact, in for an incredible night and one I would always remember. At this time, we decided to walk around on stage for a while, and I took it upon myself to go alone upstairs to the dressing rooms. I was scared to death in the darkness, but I went anyway. As I approached the top of the stairs, I noticed a smear of light coming from under the bathroom door at the top of the stairs. It is the first door I saw, heading into the dressing room area via a hallway. I was rather shocked, as I had been up there earlier to make sure that all the lights were off before we began our séance. However, I knew I needed to investigate further and discover a rational explanation before concluding that it had been caused by some paranormal activity.

There was a chance that one in our group had walked across the stage, up the stairs, and turned on the light, although I hadn't been aware of it. But, before going back downstairs and interrogating everyone, I decided to first open the door and look to see if anyone was inside. When I tried the door, I found it locked; this may not seem significant, but everyone else was downstairs, and I was upstairs, alone in the darkness, with my imagination and feeling some trepidation. Pulling my thoughts together again, I realized that the only reasonable explanation was that someone else had come up here unnoticed, unlocked the door, turned on the light, and locked it again. I hurried downstairs to the stage and counted everyone, sure enough they were all there. I asked everyone in turn if they had gone up and switched on the light in that bathroom and they all denied it. Three of them had gone upstairs earlier, in the dark, with flashlights, since they didn't know where the light switches were and hadn't noticed any lights on at all. So I went up there again, with two companions this time, tried the bathroom door again, and this time it opened with ease. The light was still on, so we turned it off, and I mentioned to my friends that if it was on again, later, I would freak out! But this was just the beginning of what was to come.

Several hours had passed, and we decided to visit other locations in the building where we had felt paranormal activity in the past. We blew out all the candles and set off for Room 101, where we set up a camera and left it running. To review what I wrote earlier, this was the room where a tragic suicide had occurred. With my trusty recorder running in my hand, we asked many questions of the spiritual world. After about ten minutes, we decided to go down to a lower floor to the California Room, a banquet facility; it faces towards the California side of Lake Tahoe. Several employees have mentioned that strange activities have happened there, such as chairs moving, silverware turning up in the wrong location after having been set, and shadowy figures sometimes seen out of the corners of their eyes.

It is a large banquet room that can hold about a hundred people comfortably, with a panoramic view of the Lake, but at this moment, it was dark and empty.

After about an hour, we headed off to Cabin 3, Marilyn Monroe's cabin. The moon was at its fullest; it was the largest and brightest full moon I had noticed of the year. We walked from the main building of the Cal Neva Resort approximately a hundred yards to the cabin and went inside. We remained there about thirty minutes, but we didn't really feel anything, so we decided to go back to the showroom and see what was happening there. The cameras had been running the whole time we had been gone, and by this time, there were only six of us left as it was late and some had decided to retire for the night.

We walked around on the stage, attempting to pick up some activity, and I ran upstairs to the dressing rooms once more to see if the bathroom light had come on again; I was disappointed to find that it was still off. When I went back down to the stage, one of the cameramen was filming on stage, while the other was filming from a booth at the back of the showroom, from where he could view the entire stage. By this time, it was about 2 a.m., and four of us were sitting around the table up on stage, the candles from our previous séance were out, and the only light came from footlights on the steps below. I still had my recorder running. As we talked in soft voices, the psychic lady, who has great sensitivity to the spirit world, looked me in the eye and said she was really starting to feel something. The moment I looked into her eyes, everything changed. The whole night had seemed calm, as though it would end that way, even though I had been hoping that we would at least get some activity on the cameras or recorders so it wouldn't be a complete disappointment. But, when I looked into the psychic's eyes, I realized that all hell was about to break loose; I froze and chills went up and down my spine. What I am about to tell you is beyond comprehension; I would never have believed it if we didn't have documented proof from the cameras and cassette recordings. Because of that, I have evidence of what happened next.

The psychic began walking towards the back of the stage; you could have heard a pin drop, with the three of us sitting silently at the table in total darkness. Then, all of a sudden, she began sobbing. Speechless, we watched her every move. I tried not to show it but I was so afraid that I just wanted to run out of there; my heart was pounding in my chest and I could feel an evil presence lurking. Despite the darkness, I could make out the fear in the faces of the others, and I truly believe that if I hadn't been frozen to my seat, I would have escaped. Then the psychic went from sobbing uncontrollably to incredible fear; all eyes were on her as she got louder and louder. There was so much terror in the air, you could have cut it with a knife. Suddenly, she shot towards us like a lightening bolt and slammed herself down in her chair. I yelled, "ARE YOU OK?"

"NO!" she screamed.

I said, "do you feel something?"

"YES, IT'S HERE!" she screamed. Then it fell silent again and I felt a surge of energy come over me as if a gust of wind had gone through my body. In a flash, the table jolted up off the ground, recorders and candles flying everywhere, and then it came crashing down with force on two of the members around the table. I will never forget that scene of how everything on the table lifted up and fell off, as the table shot off the ground. We had to pull the table off the man and woman on the opposite side, who were in shock; the woman was crying. Luckily, no one was hurt, but the shock and fear were debilitating. I was trembling and in disbelief of what had just happened. It was a very heavy table, and there was no way that any one of us could have thrown it up into the air like that. At the same time, I felt sorry that the people who had left the séance early had not witnessed the amazing event. Despite being scared to death at the time, I felt very fortunate to have been there to experience it; it was what I had been waiting for.

Here is the table that flipped over by itself. I have no explaination of how it happened. I will never forget it for as long as I live.

Chapter 16
DESTINATION BODIE

For some time, I had wanted to take another trip to Bodie, a preserved ghost town a few miles south of Bridgeport, California, on State Route 395. The last time I was there, several years ago, my son and daughter were visiting from Ohio. At that time, I had not yet cultivated my interest in the paranormal and the history of the area, but it had been on my mind as a prime destination to revisit. I had hoped to be able to gather a group of friends that would have the time and inclination to take the road trip with me. I mentioned this to my good friend Sharky, who is usually game for an adventure, and he agreed to be the driver and to take care of the accommodations. We decided to wait until late spring, when most of the snow would have melted and the weather warmed up, since Bodie, although usually open year round, is at an elevation above 7,000 feet.

About a month before, we finally agreed upon a date in May, Mothers' Day weekend 2009. By that time, we still hadn't managed to increase the size of our group, so it seemed it would just be the two of us. But, on the Friday evening before we planned to leave, Sharky ran into a good friend of ours, Victoria, at a Birthday party. He told her about the trip we were taking and invited her to come along. Despite the short notice, she happily accepted, stating that, as the weather was so fabulous, it would be a wonderful weekend for a road trip!

For those of you who are wondering what we were thinking, gallivanting off over Mothers' Day, I feel I should tell you that all three of us had lost our mothers in the past few years and that we would always hold them very dearly in our hearts. Sharky picked us up in the morning and we set out at 9:30 a.m.. The drive from North Lake Tahoe to Bridgeport takes roughly three hours, and we hoped to arrive in Bodie around lunch time. Victoria had packed us a lunch and we had plenty of water, since there would be nothing available way out there in the boonies.

It was a beautiful day, promising to be in the low 70s, and not a cloud in the sky. We all live in California but very close to the Nevada state line, so we quickly crossed over into Nevada at Crystal Bay and continued on State Route 28 through Incline Village and around the eastern shore of Lake Tahoe. Then we joined Hwy 50 at Spooner Summit, made the descent to Carson City, and headed south on 395. Passing Washoe Lake, we continued through the lush and scenic farm land of the Carson Valley with the backdrop of the snow-capped Sierras to our right. We stopped to fuel up in Minden, the least expensive gas in the area and grabbed some coffee for the road. At that point, we felt that our adventure had really begun, as we were heading toward a road less traveled (by us anyway) and outside of our usual territory.

We continued on twenty miles or so through the Pine Nut Mountains to Topaz Lake and crossed the state line back into California again. From that point, the landscape becomes green and is spotted with small ranches, and the way is lined with grand trees near the small historic town of Colville. Down the road a few miles is another small town, Walker; both towns were established in the mid 1800s and are nestled in Antelope Valley, sheltered by the Eastern Sierras.

Just south of Walker, we entered the West Walker River Canyon. The road follows the exciting, boulder-strewn, white water for about fourteen miles through a narrow canyon, dissecting the north sloping Antelope Valley, then past the Devil's Gate Summit and onward through the huge, lush, green meadows surrounding the town of Bridgeport. There was breathtaking scenery in every minute of our drive, so the time flew by and it seemed that we had arrived in no time at all.

We decided to continue on from Bridgeport and head straight for Bodie; this was a ghost-hunting trip after all. We would return and check into the motel later. The turnoff for Bodie is about six miles south of town and then a thirteen-mile drive off the highway. Fortunately, the road is now mostly paved, apart from the last three miles or so, but it was a comfort knowing we were traveling in a four-wheel drive vehicle. Who was to know what the wind and weather had done to the condition of the road over the next hill? As we crested the final hill, it came into sight, our ultimate destination, the abandoned gold mining town of Bodie.

This is part of the ghost town of Bodie, California. Lots of murders took place here in the booming 1800s.

Chapter 17
BODIE TOWN

Many stories have been told about Bodie and its history. However, due to the town's lack of record keeping and the fires of 1892 and 1932, no one really knows exactly how this town came to be. So, here I go with a brief overview of the history as I have read it: William S. Bodey first discovered gold there in 1859. Yes, the spelling is different, and we can only speculate why; some have thought it may have been an error made by the town's sign writer, but who knows for sure? A mill was established in 1861, opening with just twenty miners and resulting in the town's growth to in excess of 10,000 residents by 1880. The mines produced over $35 million in gold and silver, and the town was once notorious for being the wildest town in the West. A young San Francisco girl in preparation to leave for Bodie was quoted as saying "Goodbye God, I'm going to Bodie!" It is said that there were at least sixty-five saloons, including many "houses of ill repute," gambling halls, and opium dens. The mixture of money, gold, and alcohol often proved to be a deadly combination, resulting in the murder of at least one man a day. Eventually, production from the mines dwindled, and it became too expensive to continue. That, combined with the catastrophic 1892 fire, didn't give the majority of the population much reason to stay. Bodie became a state park in 1964, and the 200 or so remaining buildings have since been standing in a state of "arrested decay."

So here we were, on the final stretch of road, to our left the expanse of Bodie cemetery rising up the hill behind a small iron gate and Bodie town a little forward and to our right, surrounded by rolling golden hills and the deepest blue sky I have ever seen. Up beyond the town and overlooking everything is the mill where it all began. We parked and looked for Sharky's friend, a female work colleague he had arranged to meet there; she is a keen photographer and also interested in the paranormal. We easily found her in the small parking area and set off on our exploration of the town. It truly feels like going back in time. At first, we each set off in different directions to do our own investigation, peering in windows and looking at various buildings. I switched my cassette recorder on and had a running commentary going; we were all taking photographs. After about forty-five minutes, we found each other again and decided it was a good time for our picnic, so we headed back to the cars. After lunch, we paired up; Victoria and I took off in one direction, and Sharky and Vanessa the other. There were a few other visitors around, but it wasn't busy by any means; there was plenty of space to separate us from the other people.

Even though it was a clear day and fairly warm, the wind did begin to pick up and eventually it became extremely windy. I started feeling doubtful, because it was the middle of the day and so windy that we might not get any paranormal activity at all. I had really wanted to go there after dark, but the park closes at 4 p.m., so that hope had been laid to rest. Anyway, we carried on and it was really enjoyable wandering around looking at all the old buildings and discussing what it might have been like living there and how bleak the winters must have been at an elevation of 7300 feet, cut off from the rest of the World. One of the first buildings we looked in was the church. As soon as I walked up to the doorway, I felt a strange energy. I peered in the doorway, noticing the podium where the clergyman would have stood and took some pictures. In the schoolhouse, there are still math problems written up on the chalkboards, and it is easy to imagine the room filled with children and the teacher standing before them. It looks as though everyone just got up and vanished, and time stood still in an instant; it gave me quite an eerie feeling. Furniture still remains inside decaying homes, thick white dust covering worn mattresses and tables, plates, and rusting food cans still upon them, with weathered wallpaper peeling off in large curls. The undertaker's shop is full of coffins, both large and small, and in a separate shed behind it, there is a hearse, actually a horse-drawn carriage, which we could only see by peering through knot holes in the wood. Victoria told me she felt a strong presence there, so I pressed my camera up against the weathered wood and took some pictures from different angles.

The whole town has an acrid smell; we could not determine if it was emanating from the buildings or just the natural aroma of the desert flora, but it was strange and different.

By this time, I had taken a lot of pictures and was rather disappointed that I had not noticed any orbs. In my mind, I was still putting it down to the fact that we were there during the day (not at night).

The inside room of the old Bodie School. Left as it was from a long time ago.

This is the mine shaft at Bodie Ghost Town. I got some (evps) here.

Chapter 18
BODIE CEMETERY

As we stood there in the middle of town, we could see the cemetery, about a quarter of a mile away, up on a hill, and so we decided to go there next. We made our way back through the parking lot, across the road, and up the hill to the cemetery gate. Before we entered the small iron gate, we turned to look back at the view; the entire town of Bodie is visible from there, encircled by sage brush and pale gold rolling hills as far as the eye can see. To the west, the snow shrouded crags of the Sierras rise up as a backdrop, an awesome sight against the azure sky.

The cemetery has around eighty tombstones of people from all over the World who came here to try and strike it rich. We noticed graves belonging to people from Ireland, Scotland, England, and other parts of Europe, as well as Canada and Brazil. Many were children.

It was apparent from reading the headstones that there was a lot of tragedy and heartache in those times and that it must have been a tough life for those not amongst the few that actually became wealthy. Looking over at the tailing piles above town, I imagined the horror of being a worker down in one of those mines, toiling away with the imminent danger of cave-ins and lack of oxygen. Walking around, I stopped at various gravesites to have a few words with the people who had died and were buried there; my cassette recorder had been running since the moment we had arrived in Bodie. Then I came upon a headstone inscribed with the name "John Dechambeau" 1825 to 1918, a man who had lived through both the Civil War and World War One. I asked John if he would speak to me and proceeded to talk to him for several minutes. I realized that I only had a few more minutes of tape left, as I said, "John, can I help you?" The reason I mention John to you, and do not go into detail about the others, is because when I played back the tape in the motel room that night I heard something amazing.

While in the cemetery Victoria and I initially wandered off in different directions. While I was talking to John, Victoria was seated on the ground taking a picture of a grave about twenty-five yards away from me, and there was no other (living) person around. Late that night, alone in the dark, quietly playing back my cassette recorder I heard myself ask, "John, can I help you?" then a different male voice became apparent, whispering and raspy, pleading "Heeelp meee!..." The shock of hearing it gave me such a chill, but at the same time, I was excited, ecstatic, actually, and couldn't wait to tell the others, who were by that time sleeping soundly.

Up until then, I had pretty much convinced myself that we wouldn't get any evidence of the paranormal during a daytime investigation, which made this discovery all the more special. There is no earthly explanation as to how those words got on my tape. It is amazing that a cassette recording can pick up a different frequency, just like a dog can hear a certain type of whistle that cannot be detected by the human ear. I truly believe that "John" reacted to my question and, after I heard his voice, thought about him more and more and felt helpless and saddened that I truly had no way of helping him.

We headed down from the cemetery and crossed paths with Sharky and Vanessa who had been exploring the town all this time. They were on their way to see the cemetery, while Victoria and I had decided to find the jailhouse, which we had not seen on our earlier tour of the streets. We found it on our map and headed east on Prospect Street; it was a few hundred yards on, behind a small hill, which creates a nice buffer zone between it and the "law abiding" section of town. The only other building there, on King Street, is the livery stable and blacksmith's shop right next door. I was surprised to see how small the jailhouse building is, just a small shack really and, except for the bars on the windows, indistinguishable from many of the other buildings in town. It seems to me that it probably couldn't hold more than about ten "guests" at a time. With the size and notoriety of the town, it appears inadequate, although perhaps the $5 bail was easy to come by in those times! I imagined myself locked up there during a frigid winter or a blazing hot summer, with the stench of the other inmates, horse manure, and swarms of flies, thinking the discomfort and anguish would have become unbearable. Certainly, I thought, a prime place to capture some sort of imprint from the past, but it didn't happen on this visit, either on camera or cassette recording.

We continued walking on a circular route to Main Street on which we headed west back in the direction of town. About half way between King and Union Streets, we came across the Bodie Bank, or at least where the bank had once been. It had miraculously survived the fire of 1892, but was not so lucky during the 1932 fire. After the second fire, all that was left standing was the brick shell of the bank vault and the ornate safe inside, its contents still intact. The bank was certainly a major center of activity with people coming and going constantly. J. S. Cain who purchased the bank in 1890 was a large investor in the town and had dealings with many of the business owners. It was surely a great temptation for the "bad men of Bodie" to lurk around; I wonder how many residents were mugged or even killed on their way home from the bank?

As it turned out later, the bank vault had produced the most powerful electronic voice phenomenon (EVP) of our trip. While Victoria and I had been reading the history and looking around the vault, my cassette recorder, which I had placed on a ledge, kept recording. Since the wind was still howling, I had set the recorder in a sheltered spot, hoping that our voices wouldn't be contaminated by the sound of the wind. There were no other people in our vicinity, just Victoria and I talking about life in Bodie.

After we had returned home, and I had the time to listen to all of my recordings, I heard this fantastic EVP. Victoria was speaking to me, and then there was a pause before I spoke. During our pause, a third voice had been recorded, consisting of a full sentence, completely out of context with our conversation. It was a raspy, drawling male voice that clearly said, "Oohh, I think I missed that one—Mhh!" It was definitely not one of us; there were no other people there, and the words were not connected to our discussion. Do you think it could have been one of the "bad men," perhaps thwarted out of a thieving opportunity on an unsuspecting bank customer?

This is part of the Bodie Cemetery.

Chapter 19
MASONIC

It was almost time to leave Bodie and head to our next destination. I was really determined to continue east on a four-wheel drive road out of Bodie to Aurora, Nevada, another ghost town about three miles from the California border. I knew it had a cemetery, and I wanted to be there after dark; it is not a state park, so there would be no time restrictions. Victoria thought we should check with the rangers at Bodie, first, regarding the condition of the road, and get an estimated driving time. We discovered that, although it was not so far, a high-clearance vehicle was necessary and that it would take forty-five minutes to an hour to get there. We said goodbye to Vanessa, who wanted to look around Bodie a bit longer and discussed it with Sharky, since he was the driver. We decided to go. About half a mile along the rough trail, we came across a huge rut, which Sharky probably could have maneuvered around, but we made the decision to turn back instead, in case we came across something impassable farther along. Better to be safe than sorry, we all agreed, but I was disappointed.

So, we drove back to Bridgeport and took a right on Hwy 182, past the Bridgeport Reservoir. Shortly thereafter, we spotted the "Masonic" sign. Masonic, another abandoned mining town, is miles along another dirt road, which starts out quite wide and smooth and is certainly not as rough as the Aurora road. Eventually, it narrows to one vehicle's width with endless switchbacks, and we really started to feel that we were in the middle of nowhere and that, if something bad happened, no one would find us for days. The scenery was really beautiful, hill after rolling hill of Pinion Pines, and i below us, a huge flat valley, surrounded by mountains, with what looks like a dormant volcano right smack in the center of it.

Fortunately, we didn't come face to face with another vehicle on that road. I have no idea how we could have got around each other; there was nowhere to go and a drop-off on one side in places. After about an hour of driving, we arrived at Masonic, tucked down in a small creek canyon. There is not really much there, just a few old mine shafts on the side of the hill and a plaque telling some of the history, but we had fun poking around and hiking up the hill behind it to look at the views. The plaque read something like this: "Gold was discovered in Masonic in 1860, by J. S. Phillips from Pittsburgh, Pennsylvania, but tragically his broken body was soon to be discovered at the bottom of a mineshaft." Was it an accident or was it treachery? That is the question I asked J.S., but I'm sorry to say, the ghosts of Masonic did not give up any of their secrets to me that day.

It was quicker to go on than to turn back in the direction we had come, so we continued on that road, wondering at which point we had crossed over into Nevada. The map indicated that we would eventually reach a different stretch of Hwy 182. As we descended, the dirt road flattened out and became wider, and then there were creeks flowing through lush meadows and the occasional fisherman, so we knew we weren't far from civilization. It was a relief to be back on the smooth tarmac again, as we headed south on 182, noticing the "Welcome to California" sign as we crossed back in and headed the few miles back to Bridgeport; it was almost dusk by the time we checked into our motel.

This is the outskirts of the ghost town Masonic. Lots of gold and tragedy lie here.

This is the old mining town of Masonic just outside of Bridgeport, CA.

Chapter 20
BODIE VICTORIAN HOTEL (BRIDGEPORT)

Bridgeport is a small town, the main street of which is a short stretch of Hwy 395, containing an assortment of small shops, motels, restaurants, and coffee shops, many of them adorned with "Welcome Fishermen" banners.

Despite this being a Saturday evening, business was slow and all the inns had vacancy signs, a reality of our current economy, I'm sure. The town is surrounded by National Forest land, an unspoiled outdoor-recreation playground filled with pristine lakes, rivers, streams, and natural hot springs. It sits at the edge of a great, lush, green valley of fertile, open-grazing land, sheltered by the snowcapped mountains of the Eastern Sierras. We got settled into our room, which was clean and comfortable, our door opened toward a well-kept green lawn with flowers and a pleasant seating area canopied by giant oak trees. The back of the room has a window looking out onto a side street, across from which stands the old Mono County Court House, built in 1880. We soon found out, to our dismay, that a loud bell in the courthouse tower clangs its announcement to the town every hour, which gave us momentary misgivings about our choice of motel. Our appetites quickly took over, and finding a good place to eat was higher on our list of priorities, so we forgot about it and went in search of dinner. Later on, as we were having a nightcap in a bar across the street, we mentioned the bell and were informed that it gets switched off from 9 p.m. to 9 a.m., so we instantly felt ensured of a more restful night.

On arriving in town, I asked Sharky and Victoria not to mention to anyone that we were ghost hunters, as the locals might think we were crazy! So, while we were having our nightcap, we quietly discussed the events of the day and what to do next. There were a couple of local guys down at the other end of the bar and a nice young woman working behind the bar. I can't remember exactly how it happened, as we had been trying to be covert, but eventually the bartender got involved in our conversation. I think that while I was in the restroom Sharky may have mentioned that I was doing research for a book or a documentary and that's what got it started. I'm calling the bartender Chloe; I can't remember her real name at this moment and, anyway, I don't wish to use it for privacy reasons and in case I don't get what she told me exactly correct. Here is her story as I interpreted it.

Chloe is the bartender who was working the night we stopped in. The bar is in the same building and connected to a coffee shop next door, where we had our breakfast the next day. Chloe told us that, as well as bartending, she was also in charge of renting rooms in the Hotel down the street, the Bodie Victorian Hotel. History tells us that the hotel was once a brothel in Bodie and, when it became a ghost town, the building was moved to Bridgeport and renovated. Chloe said that the hotel is definitely haunted and that she has experienced it firsthand. I believe that the owner of the bar and coffee shop also owns the Bodie Victorian, which is separated from the other building by an alley. Anyway, Chloe told us that she was once allowed to stay in the hotel while she was waiting to move into an apartment she would be renting. When she was staying there, there were no other guests in the hotel, and the owner, who lived in an apartment downstairs, was away on vacation; Chloe was completely alone. She said that the ghosts constantly played tricks on her, specifically with the lock on her door. Sometimes she couldn't open the door and, other times, it would fly open for no reason at all, and she would hear strange noises during the night. She was so terrified by these happenings that, even to this day, she cannot bear to step inside that hotel. Apparently, in the 1930s, a young couple stayed in Room Number 1, which overlooks the main street. The husband was down below, crossing the street, while the wife watched him from the window. Tragically, the husband was hit by a truck and killed instantly, and the wife so traumatized that she jumped from the window of the room killing herself. Legend has it that a "lady in white" walks the hallways of the Bodie Victorian Hotel at night.

Chloe was so nice and her stories so interesting that we said we should have stayed in her hotel this night, especially since the hotel was completely empty. By that time, it was too late to switch from the motel, but Chloe kindly offered us some room keys so that we could take a look for a future occasion. I gladly accepted, but Sharky and Victoria didn't want to go; they were feeling a little afraid I think. I didn't want to let this opportunity pass me by, so I ran across the street to get my camera and cassette recorder from our motel and headed into the Bodie Victorian. The front door was unlocked, and I felt as if I had stepped back in time as I walked in. The dimly lit front room is full of Victorian antique furniture, artifacts, and old pictures on the walls. At the rear of the room, a narrow, rickety staircase covered in red carpet rises, right to left, up to the second floor. I gingerly made my way up the creaking staircase, which seemed flimsy and unsafe; a cold feeling made me want to turn and run out of there as quickly as possible, but I didn't want to have to face Sharky and Victoria and tell them I had been too afraid to go in. Each step I took felt spongy and made noise, and I was afraid of falling through and gripped the handrail tightly. I made it up the uneven stairway into the gloom of the hallway above and looked up and down at the row of doorways. I turned left to find Room Number 1, which I already knew overlooked the street.

A little voice in my head said, "Go back and get Sharky and Victoria" but in my heart, I knew I must overcome my fears. I slowly unlocked the door and tried the light switch—it didn't work, then I remembered that there were individual breakers for the rooms, which were not switched on as the rooms had no occupants. It took a moment for my eyes to adjust to the darkness; then I realized I could see shapes of furniture from light entering from the hallway and from the street lights outside the window. I took a deep breath, telling myself I was crazy for doing this alone, then stepped over the threshold into the room. It was eerily quiet and shadowy; I could make out the small bed with the ornate metal headboard and the antique furniture, everything from the 19th century.

I took pictures and spoke into my faithful companion, the cassette recorder, trying to keep my fears at bay. I stood at the window where the lady had plunged to her death and instantly felt as if all the oxygen was being sucked from my lungs, and I gasped for air. I was trembling all over and, for the first time, felt frozen in place. For a few seconds, I was paralyzed by fear and could not have run away even if I had tried. I knew in my heart that whatever was there did not want me there, so once I had pulled myself together and was able to move, I hurried out of there and locked the door behind me. Then I noticed my camera battery had died, so I headed back to the safety of the bar and my friends, but didn't tell them what had happened. I guess I didn't want to hear them say I was imagining things and, more importantly, I wanted them to go back in there with me!

As I reentered the bar, Victoria and Sharky looked at me expectantly, but I said nothing except that my camera batteries had died and that I needed to go to the motel room to get fresh ones. I handed the room keys to Victoria who immediately said she would go with me, and Sharky agreed. I think their curiosity had got the better of them while they were sitting there. I was secretly very happy to hear that I wouldn't have to go back alone, as there were more rooms to explore and I had no intentions of giving up now!

We had a look around the foyer area of the hotel together and made our way up the treacherous staircase to the second floor. Victoria was holding the keys, and she instinctively headed for Room Number 1. I don't know why for sure, maybe it was because of the chronological order, or maybe she was drawn to it. I held back and let her go ahead and try the door. This time, the key wouldn't turn at all, she jiggled it for a minute but to no avail, and as we turned to go and try another door, the door of Room 1 just opened. It was really bizarre, and Victoria refused to be the first person to go inside, so we all went in together in a kind of huddle, looked around, and I took more pictures; and then, no one wanted to be the last one left in the room. Then we had a problem, the door would not lock; Victoria kept trying as we continued off down the hallway. Eventually, she left it closed but not locked and hurried to where we were, not wanting to be left alone. We entered the next room on the other side of the hallway, the furnishings here were different, but still very Victorian. As we stepped into the room, we heard a strange tapping sound that really made us nervous. It turned out that, when one of us stepped on a certain floorboard, it created a vibration that caused the mirror on the dresser to tap. There was an explanation for it, but it was still extremely creepy. We looked in another room and then the final one. We had been given four room keys in all. The last room we looked in had three beds, unlike the others, which had contained only one bed each. This would have been the perfect room for us to stay in. There was a main room with two beds and an anteroom beyond, shrouded by thick, red-velvet drapes, with cords and tassels hanging down, containing the third bed. Victoria was very concerned about locking up Room Number 1 before we left. We had promised Chloe that we would leave everything as we found it and make sure all the rooms were locked. She did not want us to make it necessary for poor Chloe to have to come into the hotel that scares her so much, so we headed back over there to try again. It still wouldn't lock, so we realized that we would have to go back inside to see if there was a button on the back of the knob we could turn. Victoria didn't want to go in first, so I did, and the others followed closely. None of us wanted to go in at all, but we did it for poor Chloe's sake. We were able to lock it from the inside; we closed the door, and it remained locked, thank goodness, and after all that excitement, we decided it was time to go.

We returned the keys to Chloe and thanked her and she proceeded to tell us about the haunting of the women's bathroom at the bar. She had gone in there one night and had seen a tall, thin man in black with a black hat, facing towards the wall. When she went to get help, the man had disappeared, and there was only one way out of the bar. Victoria, who needed to use the ladies room was then afraid to go in there, so we decided that was more than enough for one night and we retired to our motel room.

This is one of the creepy pictures at the Victorian Hotel in Bridgeport , CA.

It was said that a man was hit and killed by a truck in front of the Victorian Hotel as his wife saw the accident from the top window in this location. She then took her own life by jumping to her death. Lots of people believe she has not left the place yet.

Chapter 21
CAPTURED GHOST

I know that I mentioned several séances at the Calne-va Resort already, but the one that I arranged for the 11th anniversary of Frank Sinatra's death on May 14th, 2009, was the first opened to the public. I invited a psychic, the Nevada Paranormal Society, and the Channel 2 news crew KTVN, Reno. Before the guest's arrival, the showroom stage was set up with state-of-the art equipment, including infrared cameras. We were prepared for anything and everything. But time was ticking away, and the psychic who had promised to be there had not yet appeared. By this time, I knew that around forty people would be coming, many of them had just finished a special Frank Sinatra dinner in the dining room. We had a large table set up on stage to accommodate everyone as people started coming in, but still no psychic to lead the séance! Eventually we ended up with roughly fifty people, including photographers, camera crews, and TV reporters, all eager to see or feel something for themselves. I felt some trepidation; it was a huge crowd, and I was concerned that perhaps it would not be an intimate enough setting to get anything, not to mention the fact that I was now to be the medium responsible for trying to coax the spirits to come through.

Thinking back to a year ago, I focused and replayed in my mind our request to Frank to show us a sign and those heavy white doors in the back corner of the stage slamming open in response. One of the security guards at the time laughed at us when we told him of the event and said that we must have been doing drugs or drinking. Of course there were no drugs or alcohol involved. A few weeks later, the same security guard said he was securing those same white doors, which he had done for the past seven years. Late one night, he went to shut those doors and, as he walked away, the doors slammed open by themselves and scared him so badly that he ran out of there. He came over to me, shook my hand, and said, "I will never doubt you again."

Now, I was focused and ready to begin the séance, as the guests settled around the long table, their faces glowing in the candlelight as I started to speak. Walking around the stage close to the people, I spoke to Frank Sinatra, requesting that he show us some kind of sign or if he was displeased to have us there, let it be known. Then I asked the guests if they had any questions they would like to ask to someone who had passed on, or try to contact them. All the while, the infrared cameras were filming, other cameras were taking pictures, and cassette recorders were taping, poised and alert, hoping to capture images or voices unperceived by our human senses. People spoke softly to loved ones who had passed on, and a few toasted Frank Sinatra, offering him a glass of champagne. Then the Channel 2 news anchor, Bill, said to me that a shadow figure had been picked up by the infrared camera; it crossed in front of the camera and walked across the stage. It was an impossibility that this figure was a shadow, since there were no lights and we were in total darkness. A few days later, our séance was shown on the news as the prime-time story on May 18th, 2009. The video showed a transparent figure of a man walking from left to right on the stage. What really blew my mind was that this apparition lasted a good seven seconds, which is unheard of. I had been concerned that with so many people on the stage, it would be impossible to keep everyone quiet enough to allow spirits to come through. But overall, I was extremely pleased with the outcome, not to mention there was more to come.

As the night progressed, I decided to split from the main group and take the TV crew and members of the Nevada Paranormal Society to Frank Sinatra's cabin 5. Once inside the cabin, one of the members brought out an electro magnetic field meter, which measures all electrical energy in and around the area. If there are no reasons for any electrical energy around the meter, such as an electrical outlet, or wires, or anything that uses energy, then there is a good possibility that it could be paranormal. The meter will register any activity around it, if there's any energy close by. We laid the meter in the middle of Frank's bed and it showed nothing, then the anchorman from the Channel 2 News moved close to the meter and mentioned that Frank had always hated reporters. At that point, the needle on the meter register went ballistic. We tested the meter all over the room in different areas, and the meter was silent, until we placed it back on Frank's bed and, once again, it went crazy. We tried to debunk the readings on the meter as some electrical equipment close by, but there were no such devices close enough to trigger the meter. After several attempts to explain why the readings on the meter continued to go off the charts, we could not come to any rational explanation; we believe that there was a good chance that this could have been paranormal activity.

Later on, I played back my cassette recorder of the event that took place inside the cabin, at the precise time the electro-magnetic field meter went wild. I asked the question, "Frank, is that you?" And I got an EVP that replied in a deep voice that said, "MAYBE!" With the meter readings and the EVP that spoke out, we believe that it was definitely an entity. We then proceeded to Marilyn Monroe's cabin 3, but we got nothing. After reviewing all the evidence I had collected that night and watching the TV news report on the TV station, I am convinced that it was a successful night. After seeing the apparition walking across our stage and all that I got in Frank's cabin, I was very happy that the ghosts did not let us down.

This is where the ghost was filmed up on this stage by the Nevada Paranormal Institute on May 14th, 2009. It was shown on the channel 2 news station on May 18, 2009, it was the prime time story.

This picture was taken just outside of Kevin's office. When we took the picture no one was present, After reviewing the photo you can see a apparition of a man. Taken in the summer of 2009 next to the showroom.

Chapter 22
SIERRA CITY

Our next adventure led us to Sierra City, California. It's located about sixty miles Northeast of Sacramento, California. I have to say once again that the ride there was spectacular. The sky was a beautiful deep blue with plenty of sunshine. The lush green forests surrounded every twist and turn the roads had to offer. I sometimes wonder if God outdid himself on such beauty. The drive took us through the scenic route of highway 49, right through the Plumas National Forest. The weather couldn't have been better. This was Bigfoot country with lots of forests, with only a few small towns. It took us about two hours to get to our destination from Lake Tahoe. It was in the summer of 2009. Not only were we in the middle of a National Forest, but we also saw lakes of all sizes everywhere. These lakes were very isolated, with very little human activity. The lakes were so clear, it looked as if someone laying down beautiful blue carpets made them. The scenery was absolutely breathtaking. Since there were only two of us on this trip, Victoria and I, we decided to stop in the small town of Sierra City. I guess the best way to describe it is, it reminded me of the town of Mayberry on the Andy Griffith TV show, only this place had huge mountains all around.

We decided to stop for lunch in the only general store in the whole town. After lunch, we found a cozy little cabin with a rushing river that ran alongside of it. It's a place that I would love to visit every year. This cabin would be our home for the night. We still had plenty of daylight left, so we hiked up a mountain called the

Buttes. Its rocky formation at the top gives this mountain its name. This mountain is over 10,000 feet and takes several hours to reach the top, but it's well worth the climb. Since we are both very athletic, and we love the outdoors, it took us no time at all to reach the top. We wanted to go ghost hunting when it got dark; however, we still had several hours of daylight left, so we headed to the next town over called Downiville, which was only ten miles from Sierra City. Downiville had lots of history and a huge cemetery, which was a good place to start our ghost investigation. This cemetery was said to be haunted, and it was in a perfect location. It was on the outskirts of town, where there would be no human interference. At this point, it was starting to get dark.

The cemetery was on the side of a huge hill, and one of the tombstones stuck out like a sore thumb, of an angel that was close to ten feet tall. I knew the gravesite was very old, because lots of the dates on these grave markers were from the early 1800s and many of these people had fought in the Civil War. With my camera and recorder in hand, we walked all around the cemetery, trying to get some paranormal activity. It's sad to say that lots of the tombstones were damaged from either the weather or by human neglect. I felt as though many of these deceased people were forgotten, and the only thing left to tie them to this world was rotting away. Some of these people were laid to rest under these pitiful markers; perhaps some of these individuals were low in stature in life and forgotten by the living for over a hundred years. As Victoria and I moved through the vast gravesite, we came to some tombstones with Civil War veterans. Some of these markers read 5th Cavalry, with many of their deaths taking place during the war. I wanted to mention these veterans, because later on, when I listened to my recorder, I got some incredible results. What I got on my recorder "blew me away." At the exact time that I asked the soldier a question, I got back a clear message. Victoria was very skeptical about the paranormal, until she heard the tape and all the evidence; she is now a true believer, because she was right there when I asked the soldier the question, "What are you doing in the war?" The soldier replied "THEY'RE MARCHING ME." Just those few magical words captivated me This is another unexplained story of the supernatural.

We got back to our small cabin around 8 p.m. We decided to take a walk around the town of Sierra City. The town's main street was only about a mile long. We were like two kids looking for an adventure. Most of the buildings we saw had probably been built in the late1800s. The town looked as though it closed down at dark, because not a creature was stirring. At this time, it was around 10 p.m. and very dark. It was a beautiful, warm summer night, and very calm with no wind. As we approached the end of town, we noticed a small sign that read "Cemetery," as it pointed the way. As we stood at the gate leading into the gravesite, we both noticed how quiet it was. It looked like we were entering the gates of hell. It was very dark and creepy. There were no buildings, lights, or any humans anywhere. We were alone. We were in no hurry to enter inside the gate to the cemetery; however, this was our mission. As soon as I opened up the gate, we both heard the cracking sounds of branches. I felt shivers go up and down my spine. I couldn't believe we hadn't even stepped a foot inside the graveyard and all hell was breaking loose. We couldn't figure out what direction the sounds were coming from. Then it became totally silent. Just as we both felt relief and more relaxed, there came a huge crash. We were frozen in our tracks. The noise got louder and louder, sounding as though something was running through the cemetery rustling branches and leaves on the ground. I wanted to run, but I had no way of knowing where this thing was, so we stayed put. Finally it was silent, again. Both of us were terrified of what had just happened. I took a deep breath and regained my composure. Whatever had made the loud crash seemed to be gone. Even though we didn't see the culprit, we agreed that it must have been a bear. After the incident, it took everything I had to open that gate. For the rest of the night, we didn't get anything else, but it was a night I'll never forget.

The Sierra Buttes just outside of Sierra City.

The Downieville Cemetery. I got lots of paranormal activity here.

The town of Sierra City.

Sierra City Cemetery.

Chapter 23
HAUNTED OHIO

It was September 3, 2009, a day I'll never forget. I was headed to Ohio for my daughter's wedding. The wedding took place in a small town called New Lebanon, about twenty miles west of Dayton, Ohio. New Lebanon is surrounded by beautiful farmlands made up mostly of cornfields, as far as the eye can see. Since I had been born and raised in this area, I knew of places to go for ghostly investigations. I asked my sister Shelley to join me. Our first stop took us to an old abandoned farmhouse, where my dad had worked, keeping up the entire property for a doctor who owned the place. This farmhouse had been built in the early 1920s. The place had a basement, upstairs, attic, and lots of rooms. It looked like it would be a perfect place for ghosts. The nearest place to it was several miles away. The house was in a very desolate location. The structure of the house looked very creepy, indeed, and this was during the day, not to mention what it would look like at night. We decided to wait and enter the house around 10 p.m., when it was very dark. We searched the entire property in just an hour. I was really disappointed, and I knew it would be a total failure, because of the dogs on the property barking the whole time we were there. It sounds funny, but I think the dogs scared the ghosts away. I wanted to tell you about this story, because we are not always successful in our investigations. So, when we do get paranormal activity, it is very special and rare.

The night was still young, so Shelley mentioned of a place where we could go called the "HAUNTED

FORNEY ROAD CEMETERY." The story goes that there is a lady who's buried there; she was born in the 1700s and her tombstone reads, "IF YOU READ MY STONE, YOU WILL BE AS I AM, AND DEATH WILL FOLLOW YOU SOON." Some say she was a witch. I didn't know it at the time, but this night would be the most horrifying night of my paranormal history. As we left the old farm house, I thought the house would have been a great place to investigate due to its structure and location. Just looking at the place as we drove off gave me the creeps. If it hadn't been for those dogs, I believe we would have experienced some paranormal activity. What a waste.

By this time, it was around midnight. Our drive to the Forney Road Cemetery took us about twenty minutes. As we got to the cemetery, it brought me back in time to a sad but true story that took place in the 1950s. It's such a tragedy that it's hard to tell, but I feel compelled and obligated to tell the event that took place. Not far from this location, an accident happened in broad daylight. Four high school kids left school and headed home. It was a beautiful, sunny day in the early part of June. It was said that they stopped at a stop sign at an intersection. As they pulled out to continue, a huge truck carrying petro ran the stop sign and collided into the kids' car, igniting both vehicles. The car was hit so hard it flipped upside down. The driver of the truck was killed instantly, due to the gas explosion, but the kids were trapped inside their vehicle as flames slowly engulfed them. In just a matter of minutes help had arrived; the firemen tried desperately to rescue the kids as they screamed, pleaded, and begged for help.

By this time, the car was so hot, the metal was melting. Tragically, they could only put out the flames and, sadly, the kids burned alive. It was such a tragic event that it's still remembered even to this day. My dad told me this story because he went to school with these kids. He drove by the scene of the accident a few minutes after it happened. My dad knew the fire chief who was there, trying to save the kids. The chief told my dad that, in the thirty years he had worked as a firefighter, he had never experienced an accident as horrific as that one. He said with teary eyes, "I have had nightmares from that accident for many years."

I wanted to tell you this story because I was told that those kids were buried there in the Forney Road Cemetery. If I saw those kid's markers, I wanted to let them know that they were not forgotten and I wanted to say a little prayer for them.

As we began our investigation, entering into the graveyard, I noticed the moon was full as it lit up the cemetery. The sky was clear and quiet enough to hear a pin drop, because the air was so calm. It was an eerie calm, almost too quiet. It was a warm night with a million stars overhead. As I stood in front of the cemetery, I noticed that the place was small, with maybe fifty stones marking the dead. Golden cornfields, waiting to be harvested, surrounded this cemetery. We were miles away from civilization. I felt this graveyard was in a very strange place, as though it had been forgotten by the living. Trees and plant life dominated the terrain. I had to know the cemetery's exact location in order to find it or I could get lost very easily. As we began our journey, I let Shelley take pictures while I recorded

trying to pick up sounds. We first noticed several tombstones had been vandalized and turned over. I felt
strongly that this was not a good sign. Even though we
had the light of the moon, IT WAS STILL VERY DARK
AND CREEPY. I couldn't believe how calm and quiet it
was. I did notice the sounds of crickets in the distance.
My sister Shelley was about ten yards away from me,
taking tons of pictures. I don't know why, but I felt as
though my heart was going to jump out of my chest.
I'm not going to lie, I was terrified; however, I didn't
want to show fear to my sister because it was her first
paranormal investigation. I could tell she was scared
to death, before we even started, so I knew I had to
keep my composure. I was afraid for a reason. I had
been in many haunted locations, including cemeteries
that could make a brave man scream and run for his
life, but I had a really bad feeling about this place. It
was bringing me to my knees. Finally, after about ten
minutes into the investigation, I started to feel more
relaxed with less anxiety. Boy was that a mistake. All of
a sudden, we both heard a THUNDEROUS CRASH!
It was so loud, in a split second, Shelley took off like a
rocket, bolting towards the car as she blew by me in a
furious panic.

All I could do was scream, "Stop! Where are you
going?"

She actually stopped dead in her tracks and yelled
to me, "Did you hear that?"

I spoke back in a whispering voice, "It's ok. Don't
run. They're just trying to scare us."

After we finally calmed down, and after further investigation, we both agreed that it must have been a

branch that had fallen from a tree. However, this time, there were no bears or any animals anywhere. It was very strange, since there was no wind to speak of. I can honestly say that I wanted to get the hell out of there, but this was what I had come for. As the night wore on, we had read most of the tombstones, except for one that read, "Saloma Krull, born 1773 and died in 1841." She was sixty-nine years old. I noticed, at this time, that the moon turned a dark orange color. I should have known this was a bad sign. It seemed as though it got much darker in an instant. The only light we had was from the camera. As I tried to take pictures of Saloma's grave, the flash from the camera lit up the place for just a second.

Shelley screamed, "Oh shit! I just saw a red orb."

Right at that moment, it got eerily calm, so calm, that the crickets stopped chirping. It was totally silent. The next few minutes were so terrifying, I got chills up my spine just thinking about it. All of a sudden, we heard a powerful roar of wind that came from no-where; it was so loud that I knew it was no ordinary wind. It sounded like a miniature tornado. These next few moments changed our lives forever! This wind surrounded us, as though it was trying to trap us. The wind brought forth what I can only describe as the sounds of DEMONS. We heard these loud SHRILLS and SHRIEKS, as though we had opened up a portal into hell. I honestly can't describe it in any other way, except they truly sounded as though they were De-mons from hell. Within a matter of seconds, it seemed like they had us surrounded. It was so terrifying that my sister screamed, "OH GOD HELP US."

The next thing I knew, she took off running, and I was right behind her. For the first time in my life, I truly felt that we were both in serious danger. It seemed like we were living a hellish nightmare. The car was only fifty yards away, but it felt like an eternity before we reached it. We were both in a state of shock. This incident played out as though we were in a horror film on Halloween night. It could not have been scripted any better. What we experienced was not an EVP, but instead, it was several out-of-body spirits. An EVP would only be heard when the tape is played back on the recorder, whereas an out-of-body spirit can be heard at the precise time it happens. For the first time in my seven-year experience into the paranormal, I ran away in terror. Never in my life had I dreamed of the sounds we heard that night. I have to say that what we heard was not of this earth and it was pure evil. The most shocking thing about the whole incident is I got it on my recorder, including the sounds of what I still believe to be Demons. What blows my mind even more so is the fact that, once we got to the car, everything returned to silence, with no wind or anything out of the ordinary; even the crickets were chirping again as though nothing had happened. It was calm and back to normal. These shrieks and shrills were nothing I had ever heard before or since in my life. Shelley told everyone that she would never forget for the rest of her life what took place that night. I believe we will both tell our grandchildren about the night of September 3, 2009. Another interesting thing we got that night, right before we heard the sounds of the Demonic spirits, was of an EVP that said, "GOTCHA!"

in the clear, deep voice of a man. We also got another EVP when I asked the question, "IS THIS YOUR FAMILY BURIED HERE?" And the EVP responded with the answer, "THEY'RE MINE."

I believe with more and better technology of today that we are closing the gap to the spiritual world. It's just a matter of time before we will be able to talk to the dead, as if we were talking on a cell phone. I never found the kids' graves or the woman's with the threatening words on her tombstone, but what we experienced that night is something I will never forget for the rest of my life.

The old Ohio farmhouse. September 3rd, 2009.

This is the Forney Road Cemetery where we heard what sounded like " DEMON SPIRITS".

Chapter 24
THE GRAVE OF JOHN SHELBY

Since I had some incredible paranormal experiences in cemeteries, I want to tell you of another cemetery not far from the Forney Road graveyard where some strange things took place.

The time was October 1981. I was eighteen years old and fresh out of high school. I was driving on the outskirts of a town called Germantown, Ohio. This quiet little town was in the middle of the Ohio farmlands. This is, once again, another night I will never forget. I can assure you, I remember it as if it happened yesterday. It was a cold, damp, rainy night. It had been raining all night. It was a fairly warm night for October; the temperature was around fifty-five degrees Fahrenheit. I had just finished working an eight-hour shift, and I was heading home. I remember the night was very foggy, and it was hard to see the road at times. It was around midnight. I was very tired and I still had a good ten miles to drive to get to my house, which was out in the boonies. By this time, I desperately needed to relieve myself. I decided I couldn't wait any longer, so I turned down a road I had never traveled before. I pulled the car over in a location that I felt was safe from any interference. I had picked another good night to film a horror story. The rain and fog made it a perfect night for zombies to come climbing out of their graves. I saw no houses or car lights anywhere. I pulled over in front of this huge cornfield that stretched for miles. I felt this was the perfect place to relieve myself. By this time, I was bursting to go to the bathroom. As I got out of my car, I saw a small hill on the other side of the road as I crossed over. When I got to the top of the hill, I realized that I was in a small cemetery. The graveyard had about thirty markers. I remember saying to myself, "this is just my luck to be urinating on someone's tombstone." But by this time, I couldn't hold it any longer. I was scared to death, but I had to take care of business. As I finished, I noticed the tombstone right in front of me. It was at least seven feet tall. As my eyes adjusted to the dark, I could see writing on the stone. I WILL NEVER FORGET THIS TOMBSTONE FOR AS LONG AS I LIVE!

His name was John Shelby, Born 1794 and Died 1843. Let me tell you this was no ordinary tombstone. The stone read, "STRANGER STOP! AS YOU PASS BY, AS YOU ARE NOW, SO ONCE WAS I, AS I AM NOW, SOON YOU MUST BE, PREPARE FOR DEATH AND FOLLOW ME." I must say, I turned white as a ghost! I was so scared that I slid down the hill and got the hell out of there.

I decided to go back to that location twenty-seven years later. It was a beautiful, warm, sunny day, and I was with my son Colin and my daughter Danielle. We took several pictures of the tombstones, including John's stone. I must have been out of my mind visiting that cemetery at night. It was spooky during the day. Can you imagine what it was like at night?! How I found that place was amazing. It brought me back to that night in October of 1981.

I challenge you to do your own ghost investigations. All you need is a good recorder and a camera. Go to a good location, where you feel a ghost would likely hang out, such as a place of tragedy, high emotion, death, or a spooky cemetery. Talk to the recorder, as if you were doing a play-by-play sporting event, so people can visualize what is going on. Talk to the recorder, as if you were talking to a friend. Ask questions like, "Did you die here? What's your name? Are you male or female?" Tell the entity to show you a sign where it's located. Be prepared for anything, and be in tune to your surroundings. Listen for abnormal sounds, such as knocks, bangs, or voices. Ask the spirit to move something or touch you. Don't be afraid, because you have a much better chance of being hurt by the living than the dead. I have been afraid many times, but a spirit has never hurt me. The more you do these investigations, the better you become. It becomes lots more fun once you get over the fear. A good way to describe ghost hunting is like riding a roller coaster. Once you start collecting evidence, then you will know beyond any doubt that there is another world or a place I call the *other side*. So, next time you hear a loud banging noise or knock, don't be surprised if you can't explain it, because it might be from something not of this world.

Me and John Shelby spend a moment together.

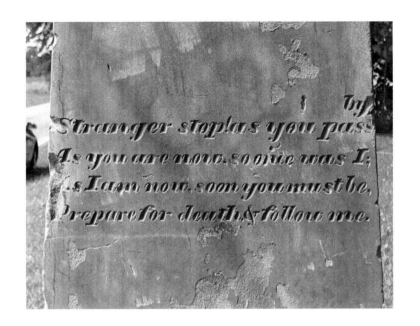

CPSIA information can be obtained at www.ICGtesting.com
Printed in the USA
LVOW081723211111

255957LV00009B/110/P